D<small>O YOU KNOW WHAT YOU'RE DOING TO ME?"</small>
Will asked quietly.

Pastel moved closer and pressed her body to his. "I hope so," she whispered.

His arms locked around her waist, and he pulled her even closer. "I've wanted you, Pastel, from the moment I saw you in that studio. . . ." His voice was hoarse with emotion.

She sighed, then linked her arms around his neck. "I've decided," she murmured. "I'm bungee jumping this part of my life." Then she brushed his mouth with her lips, softly, again and again. "I'm not afraid anymore, Will Nordstrom," she told him. "I want you so much. . . ."

He was the one who felt like he'd fallen off a tall building. . . .

WHAT ARE *LOVESWEPT* ROMANCES?

They are stories of true romance and touching emotion. We believe those two very important ingredients are constants in our highly sensual and very believable stories in the LOVESWEPT line. Our goal is to give you, the reader, stories of consistently high quality that may sometimes make you laugh, sometimes make you cry, but are always fresh and creative and contain many delightful surprises within their pages.

Most romance fans read an enormous number of books. Those they truly love, they keep. Others may be traded with friends and soon forgotten. We hope that each LOVESWEPT romance will be a treasure—a "keeper." We will always try to publish

**LOVE STORIES YOU'LL NEVER FORGET
BY AUTHORS YOU'LL ALWAYS REMEMBER**

The Editors

Loveswept ® 690

MAGIC IN PASTEL

HELEN MITTERMEYER

BANTAM BOOKS

NEW YORK · TORONTO · LONDON · SYDNEY · AUCKLAND

MAGIC IN PASTEL

A Bantam Book / June 1994

If you would be interested in receiving protective vinyl covers for your
Loveswept books, please write to this address for information:

Loveswept
Bantam Books
P.O. Box 985
Hicksville, NY 11802

ISBN 0-553-44244-9

Published simultaneously in the United States and Canada

PRINTED IN THE UNITED STATES OF AMERICA

OPM   0 9 8 7 6 5 4 3 2 1

ONE

Pastel Marx.

That was the name on the contract. Will Nordstrom, East Coast CEO of Brockman-Nordstrom Communications, the company that had hired her, knew she used only her first name professionally. What was her real name? he wondered. Was it Marx? Pastel? Neither? That was more than likely.

She was really on the way out as a model . . . or should be. She'd started ten years earlier and she was good. Mostly she'd done cosmetics and catalogues for pricey department stores. Three years ago she'd taken over the agency where she worked and stopped modeling altogether. Some said her drive was rebuilding the agency into a first-class force. As such, her reputation was good. The aura of mystery that surrounded her was due, in a large part, to her Greta Garbo lifestyle. Pastel seemed to want to be alone.

There'd been tough negotiations when Brockman - Nordstrom asked her to come out of retirement and star in an ad campaign for a new cosmetics line. She'd been reluctant even to discuss the deal, then she'd asked for an exorbitant fee. They'd bargained her down some, but she was still expensive.

And she was beautiful! Will thought. He'd known that from her pictures, but the photos had masked the hidden power she had. In person it came off her in waves. He was damned intrigued.

He was in the sound booth with the director and lighting man. He stared through the glass at her, immobile, intent.

The lighting was her aureole. She was the center of the sun, blinding, burning to blackness all around her. Like a newborn Venus, she was the brightest in the firmament.

His blood thudded in an alien awareness. What made his heart beat so erratically? He liked women, always had. But no woman had ever affected him like this. There'd been no introduction, no exchange of glances, no exciting verbal foreplay. She didn't even know he was there, yet he was transfixed.

Her every motion, gesture, look, was perfect,

without a miss, nothing blurred or unsure. She flowed with the sinuous, unconscious excitement that had become her trademark. The men and women who worked at Steele's, her agency, strived for the same fire that she'd achieved. She turned on for the lights and camera with an impossible incandescence.

Will knew that his assistant, Anchor Bliss, had seen her at a trade show. She'd accompanied her models there, but Anchor had ignored the models and concentrated on her. He'd felt she was the right person for the new account. He was right.

Or, at least, he'd been right, Will mused. But Anchor had called him the night before, saying they had an emergency and could Will come to the shoot that day?

"How do you like her, Will?" Anchor asked, walking over to him.

"She's good, Anchor. It seems to be moving. What's the emergency?"

Anchor winced. "I didn't want to upset you . . . but Pastel's adamant. She doesn't want to go to Lake Placid."

Will pulled his gaze from the tall, slender form with the wheat-colored hair that cascaded almost to her coccyx. He stared at Anchor. "It's in the contract."

"She says she's going to break it."

"The hell she will."

Anchor swallowed. "Rumor is she's selling the agency, getting out of New York—"

"Not until she fulfills the contract. Dammit, she of all people should know the drill."

"She does, but—"

"But nothing. She finishes."

Anchor rolled his eyes and stepped back as his burly Alaskan boss pushed past him out of the booth. It was always like the Fourth of July when Will Nordstrom was around. Most of the time that was good. He generated so much positive energy, everyone around him caught it. But not now. Now Will was steaming. Anchor hurried after him. "The shoot should be over in five minutes. She's really very good—"

"She'd better be at the prices we're paying."

Anchor shoved an antacid into his mouth and followed Will down the corridor. He didn't point out the obvious, that a series of tests to find the right model would have cost twice as much as they were paying Pastel. Will's argument would be, a deal's a deal. Behind his easy smile was a computer brain that missed little, and an instinct for getting it right the first time.

Anchor exhaled a sigh of relief when the flashing red light above the studio door went off, signaling the end of shooting. He doubted Will would have paused anyway.

Will pulled open the steel door and plowed into

the large studio, scattering assistants like confetti in the wind and heading right for the tall woman in the beaded sheath that hugged her form.

"Will, this is Pastel," Anchor said, chasing after him.

At the sound of her name, the woman turned, her hair sweeping like a golden cloud. Her gaze slid over him, and Will saw her bristle. It wasn't a reaction he usually got from women.

He did his own assessment of her, verifying in person what he'd already seen in photographs. Her eyes were an amazing golden color, rayed with turquoise and edged with ebony. Tiger eyes. Her skin was pink-tinted cream stretched over cheekbones that were almost too sharp, too angular. Saved by a rounded chin with a slight cleft, she radiated beauty. But why were the shades drawn in those wide-apart eyes? Why the defensive tilt to the chin, as though she expected to deflect a hit?

"Hello," he said, holding out his right hand.

She ignored it. "Hello. I'm not going to Placid."

"You are. It's in the contract."

"Well, I intend to break—"

Will took her arm. "Let me take you out to an early dinner. I have a friend who makes an Alaskan salmon to kill for—"

"How cliché." She turned back to the director. "I'll fight the urge."

She faced him again, assessing him. "Big. I've heard all Alaskan men are the same."

"Cliché," he said, smiling.

"The men or the size?"

He cocked his head, blood stirring deep within him. She was smiling, but there was a lacing of hardness in the gesture. He wanted to know why. He needed to know more about Pastel. He intended to get closer. "The observation," he answered.

"About the contract . . . ?"

"Are the women big as well?"

"Some are."

He couldn't stop staring at her mouth. The lower lip was full and sexually tantalizing, the upper one perfectly formed with a soft bow. The mouth was a shade too large for her face, as were her eyes. They gave her an abstract, impressionistic beauty that set his blood hammering. What would it be like to be caught in an Alaskan blizzard with Pastel Marx? He could almost picture the cabin with a roaring fire, twenty feet of snow outside, the two of them—

"I have to change," she said abruptly, and turned away. She strode across the television sound stage, her long legs pushing out the stretch material so that it rippled in sinuous rhythm up and down her thighs and calves. She wove in and out of cameras and cables as though they were a familiar wooded path.

His eyes never left her. He would have followed, but Anchor touched his arm.

"She's done a yeoman's job today."

Will eyed him, his lips twisted downward. "That's the idea."

"More than just what's expected."

"We all do."

Anchor sighed. Some days it paid to have the flu and just stay in bed.

Pastel pushed her way through a door marked PRIVATE. STUDIO PERSONNEL ONLY. The door swung closed behind her, and she slumped back against it, her eyes closing. She felt like she'd just been caught in a hurricane named Nordstrom. No way. It had taken her too long to chart her own course. She wasn't about to trade that hard-won autonomy for anyone, not even a sexy male in Guccis.

Not that she hadn't heard about him. Gossip had overflowed the company studio during the three days she'd been working there, and it'd been bruited about that he had a stable of women that rivaled a sultan's. She'd listened to it all, chuckled at the proper places, and cursed him in her brain. Men thought they could control everything and everyone . . . but not her.

She couldn't deny that he was drop-dead gorgeous. His thick russet-gold hair had gleamed in the lights, and just looking in his silver eyes had made her shiver. No way did she want any part of that. She needed the money from this job, but not so much that she'd allow herself to be caught in a web. She was no man-hater, but she was wary.

"Miss Pastel, are you all right?"

Pastel opened her eyes and looked into the concerned face of the wardrobe lady. "Yes, Della. Just tired. It was a long shoot."

"Sure was. Let me help you out of that dress. You can have some hot tea before you leave for the day."

"Thank you." Grateful for the emptiness of the dressing room, Pastel let Della help her from her clothes, her mind so caught on Will Nordstrom, she couldn't seem to unsnag it. That in itself was unusual. She usually had her mind on business. "Della, do you know Mr. Nordstrom?"

Della looked at her in the mirror as Pastel sat in her slip and combed her hair. "I guess I do, if anybody does. Smart man, they say. Keeps quiet most times. Steamrolls over everything to get what he wants is what they say." She pursed her lips. "Nice as pie to me. Speaks . . . and he doesn't fumble over who I am."

Steamrolls over everything, Pastel repeated silently. This job was important, the money the best she'd had. The agency was doing well. If she played her cards right . . . if she could get the girls . . . Forget that for now. Things were looking up, and along comes Mr. Nordstrom.

How could she keep her job and not go to Lake Placid? She had to stay in New York. Some instinct told her that if she didn't, she risked upsetting the delicate balance she'd achieved. She knew the girls were safe in the boarding school. The Carlyle School for Young Ladies was most protective of its students. It cost an arm and a leg, but they couldn't be under a safer umbrella.

Going to Lake Placid was just too chancy. Mr. Charm Boy would have to accept that. The sinking feeling that Nordstrom didn't accept much that didn't go his way was like a thumping in the back of her head. She sipped her tea, listening to Della chatter on about the great Mr. Nordstrom, who'd recently given her a raise.

"A veritable Robin Hood," Pastel murmured.

"Exactly," Della said, missing the irony in Pastel's voice. "He might be just right for you."

Pastel coughed, hiding the alarm she felt at having her name coupled with Nordstrom's. Would she ever be able to have a relationship? Where had that come from? She'd never considered anything but the need to keep the girls safe.

Will Nordstrom was having a bad effect on her. She wanted freedom and the girls. Nothing more. "Thanks, Della, I'll finish. I'm just going to clean my face and get out of here." In the mirror she watched the older woman hang the coral dress in the bag before leaving.

Pastel was alone. Silence droned around her. She dropped her face into her hands. Will Nordstrom. Better stay out of his way. Too magnetic, too used to power. She didn't need any more complications in her life. One chaos at a time. It should be easy to ignore him. Chances were he wouldn't come to a shoot again.

Ineffable sadness swamped her at the thought of never seeing him again. What would it be like to be in the company of a dynamic man? To laugh, dance, dine . . . For a moment she was too overwhelmed to move, then she told herself it was useless to dream. Once the girls were safe, she might find someone. She wouldn't dwell on it now, though. She'd set her life on its path. Even if she could, she wouldn't retreat. Sometimes she was lonely, but it couldn't be helped.

Lifting her head, she stared in the mirror. Brace up, Pastel. Get up. Get going. Don't back down. Slow down now, and they'll catch up. You'll be lost.

Will looked over his shoulder at Anchor. "Cancel the rest of my afternoon."

"Just like that? I can't. You have—"

"You can," Will said, and fixed his gaze again on the door Pastel had gone through.

"I should've listened to my mother and become a CPA," Anchor muttered.

"I'll take her down to Big Mike's for an early dinner."

Anchor opened his mouth, then closed it again when Will arched a brow in question.

"Spit it out, Anchor."

"Big Mike's? Do you want me to order an armored car too? His place is in one of the worst parts of the city."

"Big Mike is a friend. And his salmon is the best."

"Great. I'll just get a tank for myself, then. I'll need the protection when her battery of lawyers sues us for taking her into an area where taxi drivers get danger pay."

Will grinned at his assistant. He knew that some people in the corporation thought Anchor had too much sway over him. Will trusted his sharp mind, and his honesty. He'd been a low-level administrative assistant when Will had started working in the East Coast office of Brockman Communications. The conglomerate, consisting of telecommunications, television, and electronics had been started by his brother-in-law. Little by little Will had taken on more of the running of the company. Now he was chief executive officer,

East Coast. And he'd taken the scrappy Anchor Bliss with him on the climb.

He spent more time in New York than he did in Alaska now. Though he missed his family and the state he loved, his absorption in his work was great compensation. Putting in long hours, being active in the running of the business and the corporate interchange, was a joy he hadn't expected. It plumbed managerial, mathematical, and social skills he hadn't envisioned. He reveled in it. Every day there was something new.

Only last year his brother-in-law had changed the name of the corporation from Brockman Communications to Brockman-Nordstrom Communications. The Nordstrom family had benefited.

And all of that had brought him to this fateful meeting with Pastel Marx. He smiled. She'd stung him, exhibiting her lightning power in one sharp glance. And she'd put him off as if he were a meddlesome tabloid reporter. Curiosity, pique, and a mushrooming desire had him digging in his heels. He was going to get to know Pastel Marx . . . and, maybe, along the way she'd get to know him. He might even discover why he felt caught in a cyclone just from meeting her.

He understood Anchor's surprise at his canceling his afternoon meetings and his dinner engagement that evening. He'd rarely done that. From the start of his New York life, he'd found his days and nights choked with business and social activities. He'd liked the challenge from the beginning.

The social barrage hadn't been hard to field. People were people. The business had been a big switch from building fishing boats. His business in Alaska had involved the construction and maintenance of his own fleet of fishing boats and those owned by other members of his family. Now the business was managed by his older brother.

And now here he was, cooling his heels in a Manhattan studio, waiting for a woman who'd just as soon drop him in the East River as give him the time of day. He'd read the publicist's writeup on her as well as the dossier from his own people who screened anyone hired to represent the corporation. There hadn't been much beyond her business background. He'd been surprised that there was little on her personal life. Nothing on other jobs, family. She'd been a model for a long time. There should have been more.

She'd graduated from Hofstra University, cum laude, at twenty-one. The years following were blank up to her first contract, and she hadn't modeled until the age of twenty-four. A fluke of being in a crowd scene in a movie filmed in Manhattan, an offer of a walk-on in another. An agent offering her an opening in a television commercial. For six years she'd had some pretty plum jobs. Rumor had it she'd been offered movie and television contracts. But she'd never hit the big or small screens other than commercial spots. Her fee, though, had been better than good. Now that she ran a first-rate agency, it behooved her to court visibility. She hadn't.

Rarely was she seen socially. She'd never been discussed in a tabloid, except as the love child of aliens. Maybe it was true, he thought, grinning. She was out-of-this-world gorgeous.

She seemed driven to succeed, yet as eager to remain anonymous. A strange amalgam for someone in public life. What skeleton whistled in her closet? Who were her confidants, he wondered.

She subleased a brownstone belonging to a college roommate down in Greenwich Village. The friend was working for the Peace Corps or some such organization in Africa somewhere. Had been there for years.

The dossier had satisfied him . . . until meeting her. Now he had to know more. It had been a long time since any woman had been able to make him lose his breath. Pastel had.

She'd whetted his appetite to know everything about her, to push for a closer connection. And he had the perfect excuse.

She said she wouldn't go to Lake Placid for the on-location shoot. He'd simply have to change her mind over dinner.

He scratched his jaw, a nervous holdover from

the days when he'd gone logging on the Alaskan tree line, personally choosing the best timbers for the boats, carefully preserving the young sprouts.

Most times, he hadn't shaved until spring. The habit of scratching the nonexistent beard had become his executive tranquilizer.

He exhaled when she walked back out the door that led to the dressing and equipment rooms. If he hadn't been watching, he might have missed her. She was wearing glasses, round, opaque, almost covering her face. Her hair was tied up in one of those all-weather hats with the kerchief ends wound around her neck and tied in back. A Burberry that had seen better days, the bottom not quite hitting the tops of her ankle boots, draped her in khaki, making her all but invisible. Why the Greta Garbo façade, he wondered.

She walked fast and away from him, angling to the far exit.

"Ms. Marx." He moved to intercept her, ignoring the furrow of annoyance above her nose. "We can settle this." He took her arm. She looked from his hand to his face, her expression one of barely masked ire. He released her. "Just dinner, Ms. Marx."

"I have another life, Mr. Nordstrom, and a pretty rigid time schedule. If you have problems with that . . ." She shrugged. The epaulet on her Burberry bobbled; the thread anchoring it to the coat was coming loose. "As for the contract, you can contact my agent and—"

"We will, but I want to know why you don't like the idea of going to Lake Placid. It's February. With the holidays over, the skiing will be less crowded. There's fresh powder up north, and they're getting more." He chatted to her as they walked to the elevator. She was silent. "The lifts will be relatively free. Skating will be fun on almost empty rinks."

"I thought you were chief exec, not star salesman," she murmured.

"I'm BN's jack-of-all-trades."

"Interesting."

"I hope so."

He followed her into the packed elevator. Further conversation was impossible.

The elevator stopped at another floor. More people piled on. There was the usual jostling, angling for position.

"Pardon me, young man," a petite older woman exclaimed to Will. "Would you move to one side? I've just come from my podiatrist. I have a bone spur, and he said my plantar's warts are the worst he's seen."

Will blinked. "I'm sure they are."

"It's not funny," the woman huffed, rigid with effrontery.

"No, ma'am," he mumbled, leaning back as far

as he could. He glanced at Pastel. She was smiling. It stunned him. He hadn't thought to see the mirth or feel the shaft of desire. Though he'd first thought her more unreal away from the camera lens than in it, her smile now was beyond something manufactured for film. It was luminescent delight, filled with emotion, a restrained joy. A hot stream of sexual amusement and gladness rose in him. He smiled back.

There were mutterings when the door opened again.

"No more room," the woman with the warts called out. "I don't want to crash to the basement."

Will slanted a look at Pastel. She had a gloved hand over her mouth. He grinned at her. It was more than hilarity they shared. For him it was a bonding.

On the lobby floor the elevator disgorged its passengers with a whush that would have done credit to an exploding vacuum cleaner.

Guessing she'd try to escape him, Will curved toward her. "Gosh, you might've gotten away from me. You would've hated that."

"Would I?"

When her lips quivered as though she might smile again, he touched her arm. "Even the woman on the elevator would've given me the benefit of the doubt."

"I don't think so."

"Look, why don't we table any discussion until we eat."

"I generally eat at home. Besides, I absolutely have to be there at six, and it's after—"

"Three-thirty." He took her arm. "We'll go to Big Mike's, have a drink—"

"I don't drink."

"Water is good."

Pastel paused on one of the shallow steps leading out of the building. "All right. But I'm in a cab at five-thirty." She hesitated on the next step. "I won't change my mind about Lake Placid."

"Let's save that until after we eat." He took her arm and led her down Fifth Avenue to a side street. "Ah, there's Billy." Will waved.

His black Mercedes careered down the street toward them. The car zipped into the curb, humping to a stop, the front tire on the sidewalk.

Pastel shook her head. "Your chauffeur isn't that good a driver."

"He's not my chauffeur. He and his friends have a business after school. They move cars from place to place so they don't get ticketed. I'm one of their customers."

Pastel arched a brow. "Aren't you afraid you'll lose your car, or do you club the driver instead of the wheel?"

"Billy and his friends are honest. Billy's mother comes from Alaska."

"That's a criterion for integrity?"

"It is for me."

Will slapped some cash in Billy's hand, then helped Pastel into the car. He caught her look. "Cash on delivery. Cuts down on the paperwork."

"I see. Takes care of the tax man too."

Will shrugged. "Uncle Sam isn't losing money on Billy." Feeling more exuberant than he had in a long time, he flung the car into Manhattan traffic.

"Did you teach Billy how to drive?" she asked, bracing one hand against the dashboard. "I think you'd be more at home in a tank in the middle of the tundra."

Will nodded. "I would. I like New York. I hate the traffic."

"You and the world."

"Tell me about yourself."

"No."

He shot her a look. "Just like that?"

"Yes."

"Shall I tell you about me?"

"If you wish."

So he did, all the way to Big Mike's.

TWO

The restaurant was noisy and crowded, as always. The succulent odors were tangy and pungent as garlic warred with Limburger cheese; fish soaking in saltwater vied with vinegar-dredged beef, pork and potatoes, boiled, fried, and scalloped, mingled with the acrid whiff of draft ale and beer. Dried herbs and tomatoes, peppers and onions hung from crossbeams of the open kitchen, validating the mouth-watering assault.

There was nothing muted or implied at Big Mike's. The man himself was big, burly, and loud. The food, music, and conversation were big, burly, and loud. The salmon was red, thick-sliced, delivered every day from Alaska. It wasn't the slung-out-of-the-water, gutted-on-deck, tossed-on-a-charcoal-fire that Alaskans prefer, but it was close.

The floor was wide-planked oak that needed sanding, followed by five coats of shellac. It had a slight hitch in the middle, but it was clean, with just a hint of antiseptic wafting up from it.

Barstools were draped with denim-clad legs, tool belts around many of the men's hips. Feet were couched in dung-kicking, steel-toed work boots. Wynonna Judd warbled from an old-fashioned jukebox, its multicolored neon lights flashing. Waiters, wearing jeans, flannel shirts, and duck boots dashed among the tables, yelling as loudly as the patrons.

It was a happy pandemonium, and Pastel couldn't help gaping. Had she gone from Manhattan to the Klondike?

"Nice, huh?" Will said in her ear.

She blinked, stared from him to the crowd and back again. She shook her head.

"Don't like it?"

"Can't be sure," she said in his ear. "I'll bill you for the busted eardrums."

He turned his head so that their lips were centimeters apart. "Fine."

She reared back and smacked into someone, and the force drove her back to Will again.

He caught her arms. "Careful. These guys are big."

"No kidding," she muttered, clutching his coatfront.

"Hey, Will!"

"Hey, Jasper. How's the bartending business?"

"Same as always. More bellyachin' than tips." He bobbed his head at Pastel and skinned around behind the bar, grinning at them. "I'm Jasper Bills, ma'am. I like pullin' a draft almost as much as winnin' at Belmont."

Pastel smiled. "How do you do, Mr. Bills."

"Just Jasper, ma'am."

"All right."

Her musical voice seemed to cut through the chaos. Heads turned and male appreciation gleamed in dozens of eyes.

Will's own eyes narrowed as he stared back at the men ogling her. One by one they looked away, their conversations resuming.

Big Mike hit the bar, once, with a shillelagh. "There's a lady present. You'll remember that and keep the language on the right level. Ho, Big Will, you Alaskan outlaw, how goes it?"

"Big Mike." Will grinned and, keeping a hold of Pastel, led her to the bar. He and Mike shook hands. "Thanks."

"I know a lady when I see one," Big Mike said. He stuck out his hamlike hand. "I'm Carmody, little lady, called Big Mike by some, though it's a mystery to me why. I'm the smallest in me family."

"Really?" Pastel was so distracted, she almost forgot her manners. "Oh. Ah. Yes, how do you do, sir. I'm—I'm Pastel Marx."

Big Mike pursed his lips. "Nice name. It ain't Irish or Swede, but it's nice."

"Actually, it's Spanish ... or if you prefer, Sephardic. It was once spelled M-a-r-q-u-e-s."

Mike slanted his eyes to Will. "Decided to go for the intelligent ones with looks and instead of the vacuous ones with—"

"Careful, Ambassador," Will admonished with a smile.

"Ambassador?" Pastel felt as though she'd dropped down Alice's hole and into Wonderland.

Mike grinned. "Not exactly. I just worked for the State Department a few years back. Just about the time I started to get burned out, I inherited this from my father's cousin." He pointed toward a portrait over the bar. "Siam Carmody. I thought I'd hate it, but I don't." He looked back at Pastel. "And there's enough Alaskans in this town to keep me from being lonely."

"I understand." And she did. But her loneliness was by choice, she reminded herself, and glanced at her watch. "Are we sitting at the bar?" she asked Will.

"No. Mike will get us a booth."

She frowned. His tone was acidic. "Something bothering you?"

"It's a first, taking a woman out to dinner and having her look at her watch every minute."

"Habit." That was the only way she could handle

it. If that bothered Nordstrom, he'd have to handle it. She wouldn't explain. She couldn't. But what was it about him that made her question what she was doing? Even thinking about explaining anything to him was crazy. She glanced up at him as he looked around the bar. He was not just a good-looking man. He had substance.

Stop! she ordered herself. Don't think like that. When he suddenly looked down at her, she caught her breath.

"Care to talk about what's eating at you?" he asked.

"No." But for a moment she longed to, for a second she wanted to throw herself in his arms and say, "Handle it." She didn't, couldn't.

"I expected that."

"Now you'll know not to ask."

"Don't you ever let your hair down, Rapunzel?"

It was a searing hurt. She knew he had no idea of the pain he'd inflicted with that remark. How many times had she heard others refer to her in such a manner . . . though not in a flattering way? Rapunzel in her ivory tower. Where she belonged. Who'd want her out of it?

Will must have seen some of the hurt in her face, for he suddenly took hold of her upper arms.

"Pastel? What is it?"

She wriggled free. "Nothing."

"In a pig's eye," he muttered.

"Table for you two," Mike called out, waving them to the back of the long, rectangular room.

Pastel turned away almost at a run.

"Hey, what is it?" Will slipped an arm around her, pulling her back. "Why do you look as though I'd punched you?"

"Beats me." He was too sharp, Pastel thought worriedly. Why had she thought he'd be a country boy just because he was from the north? He was as well honed as any Wall Street financial razor. And far too intuitive and perceptive. She'd been a fool to come out with him. She glanced at her watch again. Four-thirty. Good. Not too much time left.

"You're doing it again." Will slipped into the booth across from her. "Watching the clock. I thought that was a business-hours activity."

"Not always." Grateful for the cover, she picked up the two-foot-long menu.

"Let me tell you the specials," Mike said.

"Bring salmon steaks, the best and biggest," Will ordered. "I want the potatoes baked and fried, the skins so flaky they crackle off. Make the vegetables crisp with a couple of burnt edges. Mound the Chinese cabbage high with that special lemon dressing. Dessert is baked Alaska. What else?"

"Who're ya askin'?" Big Mike said.

"That's what I'd like to know," Pastel said.

"Whoops. I think you angered the lady, Will."

Will battled his own irritation. She could fire

him up in nothing flat. He didn't like the loss of control, nor did he like feeling like the dog's dinner. Whenever she checked the time, he did. Hell, she'd slapped him down every time he'd tried to get close to her.

Mike cleared his throat, interrupting the staring contest between Will and Pastel. "About the drink order . . . ?"

"Draft beer," Will said.

"I . . . don't . . . drink." Pastel sounded out each word.

"Fine," Will snapped. "We'll get water. I'll drink your beer."

"Look, if you want to gulp and swallow your swill and bilge, fine. I don't, and won't be included in some dinosaur machismo because you're a tad off center."

Will stared at her, opened his mouth, then shook his head and gave a half laugh. "Sorry. You're right. My male whatever is taking a beating from you, Pastel Marx. And I don't even know how you're doing it." He hadn't liked the way any of the men in the restaurant had looked at her, including Mike. And he hadn't wanted anyone to speak to her, including Mike. Her clock-watching had scorched him. He grimaced. "We can cancel your order and you can get something else. That was stupid of me, and if my sisters were here, they'd blister my hide."

"They should."

"I'm sorry. I mean it."

Pastel was so taken aback at his sincerity, she blinked. "I like salmon, actually." When he grinned, she knew she was in deep trouble. He had more sex appeal than Cruise, Kostner, and Gere together. She hadn't felt so weak-kneed in years. Her heart squeezed with regret that she'd never get to know such a vibrant man any better than she did now.

"I'll put the order in," Big Mike said.

Will didn't hear him. He was lost in Pastel's bittersweet smile.

On the ride to her brownstone, Pastel rehearsed ways in which to quickly thank him for a nice evening and get across the point that it was good-bye. She had the uncomfortable certainty it wouldn't be easy . . . for her.

Sorrow squeezed her chest, but the inevitability of it all made her resolve harden. She'd had to do worse things for protection. Maybe not more biting, or agonizing. Damn his hide! He was so likable.

She'd had a wonderful time. The slab of salmon had been succulent and aromatic, the dill sauce accompaniment perfect. The potatoes were luscious, the vegetables crisp-tender, the Chinese cabbage the best she'd ever eaten. The baked Alaska had been perfect. She'd even accepted a spoonful from him, and had laughed when he'd gotten meringue on his nose. It was a lemon-honey evening. There'd be regrets. She'd live with that.

Back when she'd dated men in college, she'd always wanted romance, and sometimes she'd skated past it, almost touching. She hadn't been very popular, but there had been a few instances when it had seemed right. Not for long, though. She'd never quite gotten a handle on it.

The evening with Will Nordstrom was right on the money.

He was different. He looked like a stevedore, but that was deceiving. Rather than being a macho behemoth, he was a sleek, sophisticated sweetheart of a guy who knew how to laugh.

If he'd only acted like a Neanderthal with his knuckles dragging on the ground, she might not have cared. If only he'd belched, or picked his teeth with a thumbnail, she would have been content. But oh, no, not him. He was whole-hog romantic . . . a dream of a man . . . and she couldn't keep him. Life was a bitch.

"Tell me what you're thinking."

His voice startled her. She turned to look at him. The lights outlined his profile in Manhattan surrealism, neons flashing him gray, bronze, silver. "I was wondering how to phrase good-bye." She felt him stiffen, though his expression didn't alter. "I had a great time, but that's the last of it. I'll work for you here, in Manhattan. I won't go to Lake Placid. Nor will I go out to dinner or any other place with you again."

Silence. Air drummed around the motor engine. A horn sounded. People rushed along the sidewalks. It didn't seem real. Hard-rock reality was sending away a man she found so interesting, so compelling.

"Succinct, to the point," Will said as he stopped in front of her brownstone. "And we are here."

"Yes." She could have raged against heaven. Instead, she swallowed her grief and fumbled for her door handle. "Please don't get out. It's cold. . . ." The words died on her lips, at the killing look he gave her.

"I'll walk you to the door."

"Right."

Slush kicked up by passing cars was the only sound. Their breaths puffed out in front of them. Stars hung above them. An icy black night made for lovers who could huddle together, touch, and find warmth.

She stood on the top step, inserted her key, and turned it. "Good night."

"Good night."

Will watched her until she passed through the air lock and an inner door with opaque glass. He could see her outline, then nothing. A light went on, then another.

He retraced his steps to his car. He drove away

slowly, too puzzled, confused, and upset to move at any speed. Turning a corner, he pulled over and parked, turning out his lights. Little in his surroundings penetrated his black study. Cars angled past, spraying his with slush.

What the hell was going on? he wondered. They'd had dinner. Admittedly, it hadn't been very classy or romantic. The food had been good, though, and they'd had some privacy. And they'd talked. She was interesting, amusing. He'd been intrigued, and he'd sensed she wasn't bored. They'd laughed. They'd talked about the business. They'd talked about Alaska. He'd thought they'd progressed, but no way. He'd tried everything to get past her barriers, but she'd foiled him at every step, as though she held up a steel shield. The most innocuous questions were fielded as if they'd been live grenades.

He felt as though there'd been other people at the table, specters he couldn't see or handle. He didn't consider himself superstitious, but he'd had the distinct impression that something or someone, unseen but palpably there, had blasted any intimacy and openness.

He pounded a slow cadence on the steering wheel, disappointment churning in him like indigestion.

Shaking his head, he reached for the ignition.

A car came out of an alley behind Pastel Marx's

building. A streetlight showed the driver as clear as daylight. His hand froze. Pastel!

He idled the motor, letting her move down the street, cross the avenue. Then he switched on his lights and followed. He called himself every kind of fool, but he didn't let her get out of sight despite other cars turning in front of him, crossing between them.

She had to be home before six, she'd said, and now she was heading out again. A man! Acid ate his guts as he pictured her with someone else. Why hadn't she just come out and told him? It wouldn't have been palatable, but he'd have understood. Why the cloak and dagger? Worse, why the hell was he following her?

He just couldn't let go of her . . . yet. It was as though he'd come to the end of a long search and then been told the prize couldn't be his. Pastel Marx was more real, more full of life, than a mere prize. She was a shaft of sunshine that warmed the snows of the north, gave new meaning to the expression *snowmelt*.

Where the hell was she headed? It didn't matter, he was going with her all the way. Then he was going to ask her why she couldn't be straight with him. After that he'd forget her.

Through traffic that only ebbed to a certain level before rising again, she led him across Manhattan in a circuitous route to the Brooklyn Bridge. They could have gotten there in less than half the time if she'd driven straight east across the island, rather than zigzagging north and south. Did she know he was following her?

Instead of crossing the bridge, she turned down a side street and parked. He watched as she got out of her car and walked to a phone booth. From where he was sitting he could see her drop in quite a few coins. She talked for maybe ten minutes, then hung up. After scrutinizing the passing cars and the few pedestrians, she returned to her car and started back the way they'd come.

Will followed.

When they reached the brownstone, he watched her drive into the short alley behind her building. He parked and trotted into the alley in time to see her enter her home through a back door. He waited until he saw a light go on, then walked back to his car, head down. He started the engine, took in a deep breath, but didn't pull into traffic. Instead, he turned the engine back off and got out of the car.

Taking another deep breath, he went up the steps and pressed the bell.

The intercom crackled, then her voice asked who was there.

"Will Nordstrom."

There was a silence. "I thought we said good night."

"We did . . . but I wanted to speak to you."

"Mr. Nordstrom, I told you—"

"Let's talk about Lake Placid."

There was another long silence, then a buzzer sounded. Will pushed at the door, and it gave.

Uncertain of his direction, he looked around the narrow entryway of the brownstone, then up the stairway that hugged one wall.

Pastel's head leaned over the balcony on the second floor. "Up here. The housekeeper lives down there."

He took the stairs two at a time. At the top he stopped, not out of breath because of the climb, but because of her. She'd changed her clothes and was now wearing satiny pale lemon pajamas, and flat shoes the same hue as the garb, as soft-looking as the outfit. "Hi."

"What is it?"

Her voice was soft, but her eyes were stormy. She remained in the poorly lit hall, not inviting him into the living room behind her.

"I want to help," he said.

She stepped back, her hands fisting. "Look, Mr. Nordstrom, I don't know what you think you know about me, but whatever story you've concocted, you're wrong."

"Then straighten me out."

"No." She turned and strode into the room. He followed.

"Pastel . . ."

She spun around, and in the lamplight he saw the telltale tracks of tears on her face. "You've been crying. Because of the phone call you made near the bridge."

Startled, she backed away. "Leave," she said, her voice cracking. "You can't follow me. I won't allow it."

He strode over to her. "What is it? Maybe I can help."

"You can help by leaving." She lifted her arms as though she'd push him away.

He took her hands. "Don't cry. Please."

She pulled back, and tears began trickling down her face again. "I don't . . . not ever. Leave."

He shook his head. Cupping her face with his hands, he held her. "You hurt."

She tried to push him away. "Don't pity me, you Alaskan oaf."

"I don't."

"Then why won't you leave?"

"You need me."

"I don't."

He nodded, his thumbs sweeping some of the dampness from her cheeks.

"Seducers don't interest me," she said through her teeth.

"I won't seduce you. You can seduce me, though."

"No thanks."

"Your choice," he whispered.

"Stop."

"All right." He dropped his hands, but didn't move back. "Let's talk about Lake Placid."

She glared. "Do anything to get your own way, wouldn't you?"

"No. I'm persistent, not ruthless." He moved his shoulders as though words didn't say enough. "But I think you could use a change of scenery. Things are coming down on you. Why the phone call near the bridge?"

"Not your business."

"Right. I'd like to help, Pastel. I also freely admit that part of the reason is that I'm damned attracted to you."

"Part?" Pastel couldn't believe she was letting this impossible conversation continue. She should send him packing.

"Yes." With his hands still at his sides, he leaned down and brushed a kiss across her lips. She started, shocked by the electric thrill that raced through her at that brief caress. "I want you," he said as he straightened, "but not when you're vulnerable. When your world's steady, when you're sure, I want to make love to you."

"You're rushing your fences," she managed to say. Her world was far from steady now. She'd worked so hard to be insular, to get by on her own. He'd torn off her buffers with one kiss.

"Will you listen to me?"

She nodded.

"We can compromise on the Lake Placid deal—"

"Not go?"

He shook his head. "We need the background because it's going to be a series of winter shots. The Adirondacks fit the bill." He took a deep breath. "I'll double your salary for the shoot."

"Don't you need some sort of committee for a decision like that?" She was shaken to her shoes. The money would be manna from heaven.

"I'll pay you from my pocket." He reached into the breast pocket of his suit coat, took out his checkbook, and scribbled on it. "The first week," he said, handing her the check.

She looked at the amount. "And then some."

"I'll do anything I can to remove your barriers . . . and to protect you." When her head came up, her lips tightening, he held up his hands. "I'm not probing, just guessing. Give me a chance."

She didn't move for minutes. Then she nodded once.

"Does that mean you'll go?"

She nodded again.

"I'll take care of you."

"I'll watch myself."

He kissed her on the forehead, spun on his heel, and crossed the room. He looked back at her from the doorway. "Good night, Pastel."

THREE

Lake Placid was a winter jewel. Snow was its mantle, velvety, thick, trailing over every surface like a monarch's train. Crowned by rows of icicles, the buildings, big and small, preened in diamond luxury.

It was so exciting. Pastel felt breathless as Will drove along. She shouldn't be there. Although her staying in Manhattan all the time wasn't part of the deal, she still felt safer there. But it was so wonderful to be here . . . with Will.

"What're you thinking?" he asked, glancing at her.

"That I should've given you more of an argument."

He grinned. "You did."

"Not enough of one, or I wouldn't be here."

"Don't talk yourself out of it now. You're happy you came."

She nodded. "I didn't know it would be so beautiful."

"I thought you were born in New York State."

She hesitated. "Born and raised here, yes. Somehow we . . . I never got to the Adirondacks." Too poor, too intent on schooling and getting away.

"Another secret?"

"I guess." She looked away from him. Not once in the two weeks since she'd agreed to the trip had he pushed her, questioned, or prodded. Actually, they should have been in Lake Placid a week before. Will, however, had decided he wanted to be there for the entire shoot, so schedules had to be rearranged.

She'd spent the time finishing the studio shoot, then getting back to work at her agency. Almost every night Will took her home. He'd come in for a drink, kiss her a few times, and leave. Her initial wariness had melted into confusion. No longer concerned about whether he'd discover too much, she'd wonder whether he'd give her one more kiss, if his hands would hover just below her breasts . . . or touch. He was driving her mad.

He grazed her arm, then pointed. "There. The mountain."

"Look! Someone's coming down. Is that the ski area?"

Will nodded as he steered the Bronco through the narrow streets clogged with cars, skis and cases atop them, and people, ambling or striding along, many toting skis and poles. Snow was piled to the second story in some places, looking like glistening cotton batting in the sun. "One of them. There are quite a few."

"I didn't think there'd be so many people. We drove such a distance, through a wilderness. Just a two-lane highway with mammoth trees, thick brush, and no sign of life for miles." She shook her head. "I had no idea."

"Adirondack Park is huge, one of the largest in the country. People get lost in it every year, because they don't realize it is a wilderness. Millions of acres, I understand."

"Where are we staying?"

"You'll see."

Pastel looked out her window. A winter wonderland surrounded her, but it didn't change anything. The real world was right at her heels, snapping and nipping. It wasn't white and cold. It was coal-black and frozen.

"And it will be all right."

Looking toward him, she shook her head. "You don't know enough to make that judgment."

"I know I want to know you better. I know you're perfect for the shoot. I know we can be happy and relaxed for a few days."

"Maybe." Could that be? She'd been on the edge for so long.

"I've rented a house on Lake Placid. We won't

be too far from anything, but we'll be private." He hesitated. "Tell me if I'm stepping on toes. I'd like to help with what's bothering you, Pastel, and—"

"You're on my toes."

"You're frightened."

"Don't mistake prudence for fear."

He was silent for a few minutes, and she was certain he had once again seen past her barriers. Yes, she was prudent, but she was also scared. Scared for the girls, who depended on her to keep them safe from men who would use them to achieve their aims. But she was scared of her feelings for Will Nordstrom too. They hadn't spent much time together, yet the attraction she'd felt when she first met him seemed to have increased a hundredfold. It wasn't just his rugged good looks, but his gentleness, his apparent intuitive understanding of her. He hadn't made any grand romantic gestures over the past two weeks, but she still felt as if he were courting her slowly, carefully, intently. And she loved it. She told herself she couldn't afford to be swayed by his magnetism. Complacency could be deadly. Serenity could be lethal. But Will made her feel so damned safe . . . and so hot, so aroused . . . yet he could be as comforting as warm milk.

"Do you like to ski?" he asked out of the blue.

"I do," she said, glad for the subject change. "But I haven't done it in some time. I'm probably pretty rusty."

"How about snowmobiles?"

She shook her head. "Never rode one. Aren't they dangerous?"

"They can be. They can be great too."

"Are you cautious or careless?"

He shrugged. "Either, depending on the time, who's with me, where I am, the mood I'm in."

"Spoken like a true diplomat."

He smiled at her. "I've had to learn. Up in Alaska we don't always take time for diplomacy. Most times it's just yes or no, I want that or I don't want it." His smile became warm. "Sort of the way I felt when I met you. No questions or doubts or hesitations."

She laughed even as his words sent little thrills of delight through her. "No, you certainly weren't diplomatic that first day. You just kidnapped me, hauled me way downtown, bribed me with the best salmon I've ever had . . ."

"How could I resist?" he said, sending her a cocky look. "You're beautiful."

She sighed, her humor evaporating at the reminder that most men saw only her outer self and never bothered to find out what was inside. "If I weren't, we wouldn't be here."

"Aren't you glad you're beautiful?"

She shrugged. "It's made me plenty of money."

"You can't be that offhand about being gorgeous."

"Maybe I'm just used to what it means to have surface beauty."

He frowned at her. "It's more than that, and you know it. You have presence, a glow, a barely masked light that the camera catches. You have an aliveness."

She looked at him curiously. Did he really see that in her?

"I've heard it said I'm more alive on camera than off."

He shook his head. "Anyone who says that has never spent more than five minutes with you."

That wasn't true, she thought. She did keep her emotions, her inner passion tamped down when she was with most people. But not Will. He drew it out of her effortlessly.

She stared at him as he navigated out of the town. He had a wonderful profile. He could be a model himself. She watched his hands on the wheel, large, capable. A vision of them on her skin shot through her mind. She caught her breath.

He glanced at her. "Are you all right, Pastel?"

"Fine." What would he say if he knew how happy she was to be with him? It was crazy. She scarcely knew him. And he certainly didn't know her, didn't know the burden she carried. Should she tell him?

As if he'd read her thoughts, he took a deep breath and said, "Pastel, you should know something about me. I don't put my faith in a great many people either."

He reached the bottom of a curving road and stopped. He glanced at her, and his eyebrows drew together in concern. "You look pale. What is it?"

"Nothing."

"No, it isn't. It was something I said." He thought for a moment as he steered the Bronco onto a narrow drive that wound through the woods. "I pushed a button when I said I relied on few people. It's true. I've leaned on my family in tough situations, but not too many others. We're alike in that."

She nodded, still unnerved at how well he seemed to know her. With his simple words, his showing that he understood and could identify with her reticence, they'd crossed a bridge. A crazy relief coursed through her. "Tell me about your family."

"They're strong . . . and ordinary . . . and outstanding. I've missed them."

"You sound surprised."

"I am. I didn't know it until I met you. But there've been many times I've wanted to discuss things with my brothers and father." He grinned at her perplexity. "You remind me of my family."

"How?"

"They're easy to love too . . . and tougher than old boots. Someday I'll introduce you to them.

They can be a little overwhelming, but with my family you'll never be cold, no matter how low the temperature drops."

Pastel studied him. He could have said nothing more reassuring to her. She could grow dependent on the man. Uh-uh. Not allowed. She had to say something to halt the growing intimacy. "This isn't exactly a vacation, you know."

His smile didn't dim. "We'll work. But we can play too."

Play? She hadn't done much of that. "You and your assistant don't seem to slough off much."

"Anchor?" He laughed. "He's never known when to stop. He could have pneumonia and still be putting in fourteen-hour days."

She started to answer, but they'd rounded the last curve in the drive and there was the house. A topaz on a sea of diamonds and emeralds . . . a two-story log-framed house surrounded by glistening snow and swaying evergreens. "A Swiss chalet! It's lovely."

Will leaned on the wheel, nodding. "I saw some pictures. It's better-looking in person." He looked over his shoulder. "A nice view too."

Pastel craned her neck, feeling the heat from his arm inches from her face, where he'd rested it on the back of her seat. "Wonderful." Was her voice cracking? "It looks big. Will others be sharing it with us?"

"No. Just us."

Eyes narrowed, she turned to look at him.

He laughed. "Afraid I'll make some moves?"

"You won't. If you do, you'll be singing high soprano, boyo. I've studied tai chi."

He laughed. "You're as tough as my sisters."

She couldn't stop her grin. She was opening her door to get out, when she felt the hand on her arm. "Yes?"

"You'll be safe. You can be unafraid, Pastel. I promise."

Shaken, she managed a trembling smile and a nod. No one had ever stood fast for her, let alone offered to guard her. He knew so little about her, but he was willing to stand between her and "it." "Thank you."

"My pleasure." He grabbed some bags, then followed her up the wood stairs to the porch, which was just a raised area under the second floor balcony. "Someday you might even trust me."

"What?"

"Nothing. Look, real logs, just like—"

"Alaska. I know."

"Right."

His grin covered her like a quilt. She felt warm and safe. How *did* he do that?

He stopped, looking around, inhaling. "Well?"

She studied the chalet. "I could grow to like

this." She laughed. "You might regret getting me here."

"I don't think so," Will murmured, his eyes on her. "I think it's the best thing I've ever done." He longed to take her in his arms and kiss her, but he held back. He couldn't recall hesitating about anything like that in his life. He did now, though, wanting her to be as comfortable as he with whatever the future held. He didn't realize how long he'd been standing there staring at her until she frowned at him and asked what he was thinking about.

He grinned. "My brother-in-law."

Her eyebrows rose in surprise. "Rafe Brockman?"

"Yes." He wasn't sure if he should go on, but he realized there was no point in holding anything back from her. They were going to be spending the next five days together. She had a right to know exactly how he felt. "Rafe is one of the most hard-headed, clear-eyed businessmen I know. He's like an iceberg in negotiations, and he could convince you to give him the shirt off your back and make you believe he was doing you a favor."

"What's the point?"

"When he's with my sister, he's a cupcake. He crumbles and melts at her feet. All she has to do is blink, and he jumps. I mean it. At the birth of their child, she did better than he, and for months afterward he wouldn't leave her to go to work. He managed everything from an office at home. That's one of the reasons I'm in Manhattan. It used to be, he'd fly in about once a month, handle things, and fly back. That was still too much. Now it's my job." He grimaced. "I've always thought he was a little crazy . . . no, a lot crazy."

"And you told him that."

Will laughed. "More than once. He doesn't care. Cassie is the center of his life. Everything revolves around that."

He looked down at Pastel. She was so lovely, so enticing, so mysterious. He had fallen hard for her, and he would do everything in his power to keep her safe.

"That's your answer?" Her heart thudded against her breastbone. She thought it would break through.

"And now," he added, "I understand . . . and sympathize."

While she gaped at him, he opened the wide double doors off the deck. Inside he heard a clattering sound, and quickly put the suitcases down and stepped in front of Pastel. "Hello," he called. "It's Will Nordstrom."

Footsteps rattled on the bare treads as someone came down from the second level.

"Hey, Will," said a sinewy, tall barrel of a man. "I was wondering when you guys were going to get here."

"Hey, Dov," Will replied. "I see Big Mike got ahold of you."

"Right." Dov looked around Will at Pastel. "Howdy, ma'am. No need to fear. I'm from Alaska."

"I'm beginning to understand that's an endorsement," Pastel said, stepping around Will. "Excuse me for being blunt, but what are you doing here and what does Big Mike have to do with it?"

Dov looked at Will. Will avoided looking at Pastel. "When I mentioned to Mike that we were coming up here," Will said, "and that you seemed nervous about leaving Manhattan, he told me he'd get in touch with someone who could check this place out, keep an eye on things for us." Will smiled at her, hoping to elicit the same expression from her. He failed. "Mike," he continued, "called Dov Tayser here. He's a private investigator."

Pastel stared from Will to Dov and back again. She knew she should be furious with Will for talking about her behind her back, for arranging for protection for her without even asking. Instead of fury, though, she felt a rush of gratitude at his concern for her. Gratitude and something else that she refused to name.

She turned to the other man. "I'm glad to meet you, Mr. Tayser."

He grinned. "Just call me Dov, ma'am." He nodded to Will. "I'll just finish checking out the house, then I'll be out of here."

Will nodded and thanked him, then looked at Pastel. "Would you like to see your room?"

"Sure."

She waited until he'd picked up the bags again, then walked over to the stairs. As soon as she started up them, she realized it was a mistake to have Will following her. She felt his gaze scorching over her back. Her body pearled with a moist-hot awareness. He was more than undressing her with his eyes, he was peeling back her flesh, seeing her vulnerability. Fully clothed, she was totally naked.

"You have beautiful hips."

Her back arched as though he'd poured icewater over her. She had the unnerving sensation she could feel his breath on her bare skin. She tried to hurry and slipped.

He dropped the bags and caught her around the waist. "I've got you."

"Misjudged the distance," she mumbled.

"Easily done." He kissed her ear.

She turned her head toward him, and his mouth moved closer. Their breaths mingled.

"Hey, Will. I left some salmon marinating in the fridge."

Pastel pulled back.

Will grimaced. "Thanks, Dov."

"You bet."

Will exhaled, scowling. "I'm surrounded."

Laughter burst from her. "Just the two of us."

"And a million more in the woodwork." He released her and picked up the bags again. "I get the bedroom with the hot tub."

"Is there one?"

He nodded.

"First one in gets first choice." Chortling, she raced up the last few steps and along the hall with its balustrade overlooking the great room on the first floor.

"Wait! Cheater!"

Will reached the second floor and raced after her, his mouth curving in a smile. Just thinking about her in the hot tub was putting his blood to the boil.

Pastel raced into the far room, skidding to a stop. Sure enough. There it was in one corner, the view out the floor-to-ceiling windows on two sides showing the mountains and the snow like a primitive painting. "Mine!" She wasn't sure if she meant the room, the scene . . . or Will Nordstrom.

She pulled back, as though snapped on a rubber band. What game was she playing? She mustn't forget who she was, what her goals were. She stared at Will as he entered the bedroom, grinning at her.

Was he insane? she wondered. Couldn't he see this could be all wrong for her . . . for them? "Nordstrom—"

"Say no more. I cede you the bedroom with the hot tub."

"What? Oh. The hot tub. Yes, I won."

He walked toward her. "Pastel, what's wrong? Don't shut me out."

She reared back. He didn't understand. And she wouldn't enlighten him. Oh, Lord, why had she come to Lake Placid, agreed to spend five days with him, sharing this beautiful chalet? She couldn't have him, couldn't savor what was building between them.

"Relax, Pastel. No one's going to pressure you." She whirled toward an open doorway on the far side of the room.

"You already did."

"Wait."

"Need to use the bathroom." She plunged into the other room and slammed the door behind her. She half expected him to barge in after her, but there was only silence.

After a minute he knocked on the door. "Pastel. I'll be in the other bedroom."

"Yes," she said, her voice thick, choked. She closed her eyes, tears slipping unnoticed down her cheeks. Why now? Why not ten years ago? Or even five? She'd been ready then, unencumbered . . . unafraid.

After she heard him leave the bedroom, she opened the bathroom door. Swiping at her face with an impatient hand, she crossed to one of the floor-to-ceiling windows and stared outside.

She knew from the map and information she had that she was looking at Lake Placid and a corner of Mirror Lake. Beyond were the mountains. Somewhere up there was Whiteface. Could she chance the famed slope?

All at once she felt reckless, eager for action. Anything to stop herself from thinking about Will and the futility of any relationship between them.

Rummaging through her luggage, she found her spandex ski outfit. Far too expensive for her needs, it had been given to her by a satisfied client. She'd come by many of her clothes that way. Protected by the agency and its policies, she'd been able to accept gifts, promising nothing except a good job. When she'd taken over the agency she'd continued the custom.

Anyone else making the money she did would be able to afford an up-to-date wardrobe. She had other, more important uses for her money, though. And she didn't begrudge stinting on clothes. She would have done a lot more to keep the apple cart from tipping.

FOUR

After he left Pastel, Will went downstairs and called Dov at the number he'd left by the kitchen phone. Dov told him four other men had come up to Lake Placid with him, and detailed to Will where they all were staying and who would be watching Pastel when. Satisfied everything was under control, he went back upstairs to his room. He could hear Pastel moving around in hers. He'd been apprised of the complete layout of the place. What would she say when she found that there were two bedrooms on this level and they would be sharing a bathroom?

He opened the bathroom door and looked at the door opposite. Pastel was on the other side. A dart of desire sliced down from his chest to his ankles. He was getting used to the feeling, used to the wanting, used to being aroused a good share of the time. He wanted her . . . and most of all he wanted her happy. How could he fight her demons when he didn't know what or who they were? He wanted to love her, not just be her guardian. Maybe the two went hand in hand.

After shaving, he stepped into the shower.

He scrubbed and shampooed, rinsed, and turned off the shower. He was reaching for a towel when Pastel's door opened. Before he could speak, she was there in front of him.

"What're you doing?" she exclaimed.

Her blustered outrage made him smile, then he ducked as she threw her cosmetic bag at him.

"Wait, Pastel. Let me explain."

"You're naked."

"I know. I generally shower that way."

"In my bathroom."

"I can explain—"

"Get dressed first." She turned away.

He whipped the towel around his hips. "I'll admit it was my fault because I didn't lock your door before I showered. Nor did I explain that we'd be sharing a bathroom."

"I noticed that."

"You're angry—"

"Damn straight."

Her toughness delighted him. It would have been worth a punch in the nose to keep her that alive, that vivid, that unafraid. "We're sharing a bathroom."

She spun around.

He held his hands up for protection. "Just a bathroom, not a bedroom."

"You're right about that."

"See. We can agree on something."

Pastel fought the mirth rising in her. God, he had great pecs, and his thighs ... Heat suffused her. For so long she'd shied from any emotional or sexual involvement that her own quick arousal shook her.

"I'll leave you alone," she said, her voice squeaky, her hands shaky on the door. She paused when he spoke.

"You don't have to, Pastel. It's your choice."

"Bye." She slammed the door behind her, fighting the inner wave of hot passion that had turned her to a waterfall of desire for the man from Alaska.

Will would have laughed until he fell down if he hadn't been so damned aroused. She was wonderful. The best part had been the heat in her eyes when she'd looked at him. He hadn't wanted to scare her off and he hadn't! She hadn't rebuffed him. She hadn't run, she'd walked to the exit. She wasn't cold or uninterested. There was a fire ... and he damn well wanted to stoke it.

Exhilarated, his desire enhanced and deepened, he thought about the future ... the time when they'd be entwined, making love. He reentered the shower, but the cold water had little effect as his libido and imagination joined forces. He left the shower, toweled dry, and escaped the bathroom on the run. If he didn't tamp down his fantasies, he'd run amok in the Adirondack wilderness.

Twenty minutes later they were downstairs, dressed for skiing.

Will opened the outside door, then immediately pushed Pastel behind him.

She peeked over his shoulder.

"A dog! Oh, he looks hungry."

"Pastel. Don't move." Will edged her back.

The dog followed. He walked around them, into the house and flopped on the oval Indian rug in the great room.

"He's exhausted," she whispered.

"He's a Rottweiler," Will said through his teeth.

"He's hungry."

"Some things don't go together. Like dogs and downhill skiing."

"Let's feed him, give him something to drink, and let him rest."

"Leave him here while we go skiing?" Will stared over his shoulder at her. When she nodded, he winced. "Not a good idea. If he takes a liking to the place, he might not let us back in."

Pastel was around him before he could stop her, kneeling down next to the creature. "He's a good boy, aren't you?"

Will tensed, ready to leap. When the dog licked her hand, he almost fell to his knees. "All right. I'll get something."

He was back in minutes with two pans, one with water, the other with corn flakes and milk. He grimaced at her raised eyebrows. "Can I help it? I didn't come with twenty pounds of kibble."

"And I thought you were efficient," she murmured.

At her dimpled smile, Will was fully prepared to roll over and bark. "You win, lady. Enjoy—"

"Rudy. We'll call him Rudy."

"Has it occurred to you he might have a family looking for him?"

Pastel frowned. "We can check. For the moment, he's Rudy."

"Right." Will was glad to see her happy. To keep her like that he would have imported ten more Rottweilers.

Pastel studied him. He hadn't questioned her desire to take in the lost dog. It was as though he sensed her need for a bulwark against loneliness and the danger of intruders. He'd known from the start she buried a portion of her life, yet he'd gone along, stayed at her shoulder. She closed her eyes for a moment. How wonderful to have a Will

Nordstrom in her life . . . even for a little while.

He took her arm, steering her away from the dog, who'd gobbled his food and was now sprawled on the rug. "What's up?"

"I—I . . . nothing." She welcomed the supporting arm that went around her.

He held her against him. "It doesn't seem like nothing." His free hand stroked her back. "Don't be afraid. Whatever it is that haunts you, and I know it's something, it won't get you. I'll see to it." His smile crooked when she looked up at him. "I'm one tough Alaskan when I have to be. I'll keep you safe, and comfort you."

She wanted the comfort so very, very much . . . and more. She wanted the man. She hadn't leaned in so long. It felt alien, weird . . . and so warm. She'd been cold, wary, watchful for forever, it seemed. Lifting her hands almost in supplication, she nearly told all. Then she shook her head. "I'm . . . all right."

"You're carrying too much on your shoulders. Give me some of your burdens, Pastel."

Wide-eyed, she stared up at him. "You don't know what you're asking."

He shrugged. "No job's too big. Ask." He wanted to envelop her in his arms, cuddle her, soothe her, take away the fear, the hurt. At the same time, he wanted to undress her, caress her, bring her to furnace heat, culminate their love with a volcanic joining that would rock the Swiss chalet off its foundations.

"I—I—"

"Take it slow."

"I'm almost on stop," she muttered.

He touched her cheek, then hooked a finger into a loosened strand of hair, pulling so that it fell free around her face. "Let your hair down, Rapunzel. You can trust me." He saw the flash of hurt, how she pulled back, her eyes flickering, before she covered up. He remembered she'd seemed hurt when he'd called her that before. He wanted to know why, but now was not the time to probe. She was raw enough.

"Can I afford to trust my instincts?" she murmured. "When there are others involved?"

"I'm a solid kind of guy."

Her gaze slid past his shoulder to the animal. "Funny how the innocent get hurt."

Will's gaze followed hers to the dog. He frowned. "You have an animal at risk?"

"No. I—I guess I can't explain. Can you accept that?"

"If I must."

She swallowed. "We should go."

"I can help." He leaned over and kissed her cheek.

"I know. It's so Alaskan," she said, her lips curving to warmth.

"Yes, dammit, it is." He took a deep breath. "I guess I should warn you that I told my mother and father about you, and my sister and brother-in-law, and my other sisters and brothers—"

"Do you have a standing army?"

He nodded. "They want to meet you."

"I'd like that. But going to Alaska is impossible. This was a big enough trip—"

"They're going to fly here . . . to Lake Placid. Not my sister Cassie and her husband Rafe, nor my brother Kort and his wife Linnie. Their children are pretty small—"

"How many?"

"A few," he hedged.

"The number."

"Mother, Dad, Aunt Adela . . . she's not my aunt, she's Rafe's aunt. But we call her that—"

"Go on."

"Lars, my older brother, and he might bring Sylvie Bedmill, and her brother Little Thom—"

"Is he little?"

"Well, no. He's six feet nine and weighs about two hundred and sixty pounds. But he's smaller than some of his cousins—"

"You're making this up."

Will crossed his heart. "Honest."

"That's all?"

"Well, my sister Andrea—we call her Andy—will come. That's it."

"Are they staying here?"

"No, I rented a house for them beyond here. It has ten bedrooms, and a cook and housekeeper. My mother won't like that. But I didn't want her working when it's more like a vacation."

"Naturally." Pastel's knees felt wobbly. It was crazy. Will Nordstrom was nuts. He'd asked his enormous family to fly all the way from Alaska to New York just to meet her?

"I've never known anyone like you."

"Ditto, lady." He kissed her hair. "I want to know more."

So did she, but she didn't say it.

The slopes were thigh deep in thick powder that puffed around them as they snapped on their skis. They skied over to the lifts and got in the short line. It would be like climbing to the top of the world. The sun shone, making the snow diamond-bright, the sky sapphire.

Eager and excited, Will glanced at Pastel. "Hey!" He edged closer to her. "You don't look ready for the lift." He slipped a sustaining arm around her waist. "We don't need to do this."

"I want to," she said despite the sweat pearling on her upper lip. "It's just that I haven't skied for several years. I was klutzy then."

"Beginners' slope?"

She smiled. "Better not. You'll get bored. We'll aim for the intermediate."

"Fine." He studied her, his gaze lingering on her eyes and mouth.

"What?"

He exhaled a gust of cloudy breath. "I don't want you frightened of anything. If this bothers you, we won't do it."

"Frightened? No. Uncertain is more like it." She gazed around her at the lifts, the clusters of people. "It should be all right." When she skied away from him, moving to fill the gap in the line, he stared after her for a moment.

They got on the lift and he put his arm around her. She looked up at him and smiled. His arm tightened. He wouldn't let her be scared. He'd stand between her and whatever it was.

At the intermediate level they got off, skiing away from the lift.

"On top of the world," she murmured, gazing around her. The few people on the slopes looked like moving dots. From the crest of the hill they could see the winter fantasy. Snow, as far as the eye could see, combed with pine and fir silhouetted black on the glistening surface. They were all but alone. Pastel had the curious sensation that they were, truly, by themselves. The last to inhabit the planet. It was stimulating, liberating. She embraced the loss of burdensome responsibility. Yet she wouldn't and couldn't inhabit such a world. When she felt his touch on her arm, she turned, her face uplifted.

For a moment he simply stared at her. Then in slow, measured moves he lowered his head, his lips just touching hers. When she didn't move back, he dropped his ski poles and caught her close, his mouth slanting over hers. Rich and deep, the embrace swirled around them like a live wire. At first the kiss was light and coaxing, a delicate exploration of her lips. His mouth shaped itself to her contours, and they began to flame.

Pastel had been kissed many times by many men, some experienced, some not so. Never had she felt such rivulets of fire eating up her nerve ends, coursing through her blood. He didn't hurry it. He stoked it. She wanted more.

A voice deep inside told her to pull back. She tried, but the fire had her, consuming her. It wouldn't let her retreat.

His one hand shifted down, edging her closer. Through the spandex she could feel his aroused body. It spurred her libido to full gallop.

Lost in the wild wonder, her gloved hands, ski straps clinging to her wrists, crept around his middle.

Hoots, whistles, catcalls from those passing up to the expert run, didn't even penetrate the hot aura of flooding emotion.

Will at last lifted his head, out of breath, reeling, wanting more. "Pastel . . . ?"

She stared up at him. She tried to speak, then she pushed back, slipped her poles into her hands, executed a stem christie, and jumped over the crest.

"Pastel! Wait!"

He rushed his own takeoff, hurrying to catch her.

Will had been skiing all his life, and he'd skied some pretty tough slopes. Glacier skiing, helicopter skiing, he'd managed them all. He'd even hot-dogged when he was younger. He thought of himself as able on the slopes. At that moment training was lost. Hot emotion drove him, and he pushed off too fast, not concentrating. Almost at once he knew he was not in a good skiing line. He fought to compensate and succeeded in making his fall line steeper.

He shot straight down, past Pastel, who was now paralleling in a lazy criss-cross pattern. He struggled to get his line and balance. For a flash he had it, then his ski caught on a track, demanding ordinary correction. He was off balance and when he flung to one side to steady himself, he became airborne. Then he spun to the ground, his skis releasing as he went end over teakettle.

"Will!"

He heard her warning even as he cursed his own stupidity. He crashed to a stop with his head on the downward lie of the hill, his chin plowing the snow.

Unmoving, cursing, he brought his hand up to empty his mouth of snow. He'd fallen correctly and wasn't hurt. His dignity, however, had taken a lethal hit.

Pastel's face hovered into view as he sat up, swiping at the snow on his face. "Are you all right? I can hail the ski patrol."

"Hail a straitjacket . . . for a nut," he said, disgusted, brushing himself off. When she chuckled, he scowled at her. "Have you no heart, woman? I might've been killed."

"I would've given a month's pay to video that." She put a gloved hand over her mouth, then she shook her head. "Are you sure you're not hurt?"

"My ego is bruised. My dignity is battered. I need an ambulance."

She sank down beside him. "You're a nut."

"I said it first." He stared into her eyes, then blinked, looking around him. "Get out of the way, beautiful. We're right in the traffic lane. I'd better get my skis and poles before someone snags them."

Shaken by the endearment, Pastel tried to break free. It was one thing to be snatched senseless in a kiss. It was nonsense to be thrown by a sweet name. "May . . . maybe you shouldn't ski."

"Only my ego requires medical care."

She fought fresh mirth when he slipped trying to recapture a ski.

"I heard that."

"You're entertaining."

He made a face at her. "I happen to be wonderful at everything I do, Pastel Marx. You're seeing an unusual side of me."

"The clumsy, inept, doddering side?"

"Now, wait! Doddering? I'll have you know, I've got many good years yet."

"If you don't die on the slopes."

He grimaced. "There is that."

"You were so funny. Just like a big snowball. Bing, bang, boom." She made cartwheels with her hands.

"Wait. I was graceful, rhythmic—"

"You flopped, Nordstrom."

"Naw. I was just kidding. All an act." Entranced at her enjoyment, he would have tossed himself down the rest of the hill to broaden her smile.

"Maybe we shouldn't ski," she said, catching her lower lip in her teeth.

"Laugh. Get it out of your system. Then we'll ski."

"Falling is not funny," she said, but she couldn't hold back her laughter any longer. It burst from her. "You were so cute."

Will closed his eyes. "Please. Not cute."

"Adorable, then?"

"I live to make you laugh."

"I'm beginning to believe that.

"Very amusing."

He got to his feet, hiding his smile as he looked down to brush himself off. After refastening his skis, he turned to her. "This time I'll get to the bottom."

"As a snowball?"

He wrinkled his nose at her. "Let's go. And, you know, it was a huge boulder that tripped me." He waited for her howls and hoots, smothering a grin when they came right on cue.

He pushed off, his concentration on, his schussing even and rhythmic, his paralleling marked and poised. It felt good. Leaning forward for extra speed, he reveled in the wind, the bite of snow, the rush.

At the bottom he turned and waited for her, hiding his triumph. She'd watched him ski, and he knew he'd been good. Better than that, with one fall he'd knocked down a string of barriers between them. He damn well wouldn't let them be built again. Pastel had become important very fast. He would risk a great deal to keep her close.

She schussed up to him, peaches blooming in her cheeks, her eyes sparkling. "It was wonderful."

"Let's do it again."

"It's not too late?"

He shook his head, gesturing toward the lifts.

It was a day he'd never forget. He fell in love. No, that wasn't right. He affirmed his love for Pastel.

He'd fallen in love with her the first time he'd seen her in the studio.

He eyed her as they skied down for the third time. She was just to his left, moving better than she had the first time. It wasn't going to be easy, he knew. What they had between them was volatile. He sensed she had an enormous capacity for love. But the walls were high and thick.

At the bottom he glanced at her. She leaned on her poles, shifting her shoulders as though they'd stiffened.

"Let's go again," she said.

He shook his head. "I'd like a hot chocolate."

She smiled. "I'm for that."

They skied again after warming soup and chocolate. When the sun began to dip, they left.

Back at the chalet they were greeted with barks and snuffles.

Pastel beamed. "He's still here."

"I hope he lets us inside." Will unlocked the door and peered around it.

Pastel leaned around him. "He's lovely." She entered in front of Will, who took hold of her arm.

When the dog growled, Will pulled her to a stop. "Easy, guy. Want some more food?" He edged her back to the door. "Let's give him a minute."

"He's all right."

"Then I'll coax him outside."

"He'll be cold."

"All right. Just stay close to me."

"You're bossy, Nordstrom. Now go get Rudy some food."

"Yes, ma'am."

He hotfooted it to the kitchen. After refilling the bowl he'd used before with cereal and milk, he looked around the kitchen to see what sort of food it had been stocked with. As Dov had promised, salmon was marinating in the refrigerator. He'd grill that for dinner. In the meantime . . . He grinned when he found a box a chocolates. He popped one into his mouth, then carried the box and Rudy's bowl back out to the great room.

"This will have to do for him again," he said as he set the bowl down.

They both watched as the broad canine gulped his food, then sank to the floor, eyeing them.

"I think he likes us," Pastel whispered, speaking around a half-chewed chocolate caramel.

Will nodded. "Maybe." He munched his third chocolate.

"I thought you Alaskans were macho beer slingers."

"That too." He grinned at her. Things were looking good. They were in their house. They shared it. He had days to convince her what a winner he'd be at her side. The longer he was with her, the more he got to know her, the more convinced she'd become that he was right for her. It would happen. Had to. He handed her another chocolate.

"I don't suppose we could keep him," she said.

Her voice had quivered. He'd heard the lacing of hope and the acceptance of reality. Hadn't she ever had a dog? His family had had so many, all loved and fussed over, even the sled dogs.

"Well . . . he doesn't look too well cared for. His paws are pretty messed up. Looks like he's traveled some distance. No collar." He shrugged. "We can put an ad in the paper, but in the meantime, why not keep him?"

"We could?"

The glow of moisture in her eyes, her smile of delight, sent pleasure rocketing through him. If Rudy's owners showed up, he'd pay them anything to keep the canine, or he'd buy her another dog just like him. Pleasing Pastel was a sweetness he'd not experienced before, one that he wanted to happen over and over. His life had turned a corner. He wouldn't go back.

FIVE

The shoot was going well, and Anchor Bliss was blissful. When Will had told him he'd convinced Pastel to come to Lake Placid, Anchor hadn't believed she would really be on the mark for the shoot. She was, though. Looking beautiful, serene, and capable, she'd gone right through her piece without a hitch. More than that, they weren't going to have to use a voice-over. Pastel had read the lines, and she was too perfect to be real. Anchor was downright gleeful.

He sat in the trailer provided by the company, keeping warm and sipping coffee, thick with real cream, the way he liked it. He studied the director's plans for the next day's shoot. Yes, it looked as though tomorrow would be just as stellar as today. And the weatherman seemed to think there'd be sunshine. Great.

When the door opened behind him, he didn't look up. "Close it, will you, before the room gets chilled."

"Anchor Bliss?"

Anchor spun in his chair, half rising. "Yeah. Who's asking? What the hell are you doing in the trailer?" He didn't know the men. It angered him that they'd gotten past security.

His face was grabbed by a hamlike hand.

He struggled. "Hey!"

"Shut up." The second man, half the size of the guy who'd grabbed him, smiled at Anchor. "Don't say anything. If you're nice and quiet, Felix will put you down without breaking your jaw. How would that be?"

Anchor tried to think. The pain in his face wouldn't let him. He nodded, agony radiating through his bones.

"Now, sit down, Anchor Bliss. What a strange name. I don't like it."

Anchor sat, not responding. Who were they?

"My name is Beldor, Amos Beldor, and I work for some rather barbaric people." He jerked his head toward the giant called Felix, who stood behind him, flexing hands that resembled fireside coal scuttles. "I'm instructed to use any means to achieve our ends." He grinned. "And I will."

Anchor didn't move.

"Now, Anchor Bliss, you have a mother who gambles."

Anchor stiffened. "Not much, just a little bridge, some—"

Felix leaned over and grasped his face again.

"I don't like to be interrupted," Beldor said. "Did I mention that?"

Anchor shook his head, stars leaping behind his eyes until the giant released him.

"I don't. Now, your mother was extended some credit when she accompanied some friends to Atlantic City. She doesn't have the wherewithal to pay her debts."

A creeping horror had cold sweat washing over Anchor's body.

"I see you're beginning to get my drift. Good. Now, we intend to write off your mother's debt if you do just one small favor for us."

That night Rudy was sprawled in front of the fire in the great room and Will was sitting on the couch, reading a report. He looked up when Pastel came down the stairs wearing an Icelandic sweater. She headed out the door onto the wide deck.

Maybe she wanted to be alone, he thought, curbing the immediate impulse to join her. People needed time to think. He sat for five minutes, then tossed the report on the couch and rose, stretching. He felt alive, excited . . . wanting. Instead of his interest waning, it had grown every minute he was with Pastel. He'd wanted other women before, but none had bored to the core of him as she had. He wanted to be her lover, and mother, father, sibling . . . everything. All things, in every way he could. What was her magic? Why this woman? What wonderful sleight of hand had she mastered that she could turn his life around? He stared at the outside door and the window next to it, pelted with soft snow. If he went out there, what would she do? She could tell him to go to hell. He wouldn't go that far, but he'd get out of her face if she preferred.

He pulled on a down vest and followed her outside.

She was staring up at the sky. At the sound of the door opening and closing, she turned, smiling. "It's such a beautiful night. I just had to come out."

"Of course." When she smiled like that, he turned to jelly inside. His knees were too weak to hold him. Did he have any effect on her? Maybe she was too torn up inside from problems to feel anything. He'd go some serious lengths to correct that. What's wrong, Pastel? he asked her silently. When you look at the moon, what do you wish for?

"Once in awhile I take my little nephews and nieces outside so they can see the Alaskan moon, which is bigger than any moon in this area—"

"Naturally."

He grinned. "And then when they're looking at it, I tell them about the real men in the moon, astronauts and cosmonauts who made it from here to there."

"The perfect uncle."

He shrugged, gathering warmth from her soft voice. "Maybe not. I have as much fun as they do."

"Maybe you should have become a teacher."

"I have taught, in a way. My sister Cassie teaches music at the local school. She has all of us, at one time or another, doing something with reading or music. I like it." He moved his shoulders as though he'd just revealed too much. "Not that I wouldn't have to do it anyway if I didn't like it. Cassie can be pretty persuasive . . . and tough."

"That's Alaskan women for you." She smiled when he laughed.

"Wait until you meet her. You'll like her."

Her smile wavered. "Will, don't think that—"

He touched her arm. "Don't shut doors, Pastel. They're open only a crack. One small step at a time." He leaned over her. "Pastel, I want you to be relaxed and happy while we're here. It would be easier if I knew the enemy. You can confide in me. I'm trustworthy."

For moments she studied his face. "Not a good idea."

"Not a bad one either." When he saw her shiver, he put his arm around her and led her back into the chalet. "I'll make tea."

"I'll help." She didn't remove her sweater as they strolled to the kitchen area, separated from the great room by a large counter.

With the kettle on and sugar and milk on a tray, they sat facing each other on high stools. "Don't be afraid," he whispered.

"Too late." Will Nordstrom made her world better, she thought. He could wipe out fear, or at least make it easier to handle. It was too simple to love him. But she couldn't, shouldn't . . .

The kettle whistled. Pastel rinsed out the china pot with the hot water, then set the silver tea ball in the pot to steep. Will carried the tray out to the great room, setting it on the table in front of the semicircular couch near the fireplace. Pastel followed, roaming the room for a minute before sitting on the couch.

"I don't know if I can do this," she said. "It's been locked away for some time. It doesn't have anything to do with trusting you."

"Go ahead," Will said. "As I said, I'm trustworthy."

"I've learned that it's easier not to trust." She hesitated. "But if I don't talk about at least some of it, I might explode."

"I'll take what I can get." Will poured the tea and cupped his hands around the mug, needing the heat. He wanted to learn what was hurting her, yet at the same time, he was certain there'd be changes between them. She could feel threatened that he knew something more about her.

"I'm not sure where to start," she said, picking up her own mug. "College, I suppose. It was the best time of my life, mostly because of one person. My dearest friend, Pam Harvester, from Des Moines." She grinned. "Pam was a real farm girl. Her father raised corn. I was a city girl from Buffalo. My father was a druggist, my mother a librarian. I was an only child. I didn't know until I met Pam that I'd ever been lonely for a sibling." She looked into her mug as though she could see the past there. "We were freshmen when we were first approached to join the Volunteers for African Relief. It grew from there. We were a team all through college. Altruistic as hell. We'd solved most of the world's problems by first semester, junior year. I was called Pat then. We were Pam and Pat, the dynamic duo." She swallowed. "We didn't look like missionaries. More like crazy adventurers. Totally idealistic, we rarely looked at the dark side of anything, and our eagerness chased away any concrete view of reality. No barrier too big, no mountain too tall. That was us. Maybe if one of us had been more hard-headed, we might have thought twice."

"Idealism is sometimes the basis for real compassion."

She sipped her tea. "Thanks for that. Sometimes when I look back, I think we were mad." She bit her lip. "So many ifs. No matter. I wouldn't have missed having Pam as my friend even if I could've seen into the future."

It was as though she retreated to that time. He could feel her leave him, travel back alone, unaided. Not a happy trip. That came off her in waves. Will wanted to go with her, but he sensed she needed to do this herself. He settled back, pulling away from her physically, giving her the space she needed to relive that time.

In a sudden move she grasped his hand. "It still hurts."

"I know." He waited, curling his fingers around hers.

She licked her lips, seeming not able to get the words from her throat at first.

"We had a friend from Nahumi, a small African country that curves into the border between Ethiopia and Somalia. They'd suffered drought, as their neighbors have, for many years. When Ibn, our friend, told Pam and me about the sad times in his country, we decided to pay back some of the good fortune we'd had to the people of Nahumi."

"So you became missionaries of a sort."

"Don't get me wrong. It wasn't all sacrifice. We met wonderful people, good people, and we got a peek into the real world. That taught us much."

"I'm sure." Watching her, Will saw the sudden

trembling of her lips, the way she blinked her eyes as if holding back tears. When she turned toward him, she was vulnerable, pained.

"Why did it happen?"

Her tortured voice tore him apart. He pulled her into his arms, his heart thudding when she pushed her face into his neck. Whether she admitted it or not, a part of her sought his comfort. Soon he'd make her see that they were a great pair. They fit. He kissed her ear. "Don't think about it if it hurts so."

She sighed, making a move to free herself. When his hold tightened, she was still. "It hurts. I suppose it always will."

"Talking will help."

She nodded and sat up. He poured more tea for her. Picking up her mug, she continued.

"The September after graduation, we went to Nahumi as part of Volunteers for African Relief. Nmaba, the capital city, wasn't what we'd pictured. We envisioned goat carts, squalling camels, rickety vendor stands, hordes of poor . . . and there was that. Also, it bustled with Mercedes, Rolls-Royces, and classic Daimlers alongside the pack animals. Nahumi is rich in gems, but the mines are hard to reach. They get it out, but it's expensive and few of the people benefit from the income. A wide chasm exists between the haves and have-nots."

"There's a lot of that going around."

"Yes. But somehow it seemed particularly awful when it was so glaringly obvious."

"You could have left."

"No." She sighed. "Not really. Pam was in love, you see, with Ibn. I was never that fond of him myself. He's from a wealthy family and his father is—or at least was—very high in the government, the equivalent of a prime minister, I believe. Ibn never believed in working hard. He probably wouldn't have graduated from college if Pam hadn't always given him her notes, even written a few papers for him. For the first several months we were there, she and I worked ten, twelve hours a day. We didn't begrudge it, because over the months we began to see wonderful results, more babies and mothers surviving childbirth, some semblance of health-related programs. We drained and rerouted ditches that had been used for drinking and a septic system, we built shelters, stocked medical supplies, unloaded trucks filled with goods and food. And then . . . and then Pam married Ibn.

"Everything changed. He didn't want his wife to work, so she ended up spending all her time in his family's enormous house. I stayed because she got pregnant right away and wanted me to stay with her. Throughout the pregnancy she was cosseted by Ibn and his family. Then, after seventeen hours of labor, she gave birth to twin girls." Pastel licked her lips. "Everyone's attitude toward Pam changed one hundred and eighty degrees."

"Because she had two girls, not a son?"

"Yes." She shook her head. "Ibn came around for a while, but I guess tradition and family pressure were too much for him. Before the girls were even a year old, he told Pam they were going to be married off."

"Damn! Who the hell would agree to such insanity?"

"Nahumi is a relatively stable country with a ruling family and a Parliament with limited powers. But throughout the country there are several princes, or tribal chiefs, some of whom wield quite a bit of power. One in particular had been threatening to challenge the sheikh, Said. Said agreed to give the prince Ibn's daughters in exchange for peace and rights to mine some of the prince's tribal lands."

Will hauled her against his chest as though he could take her pain into him and give her peace. He couldn't believe what she and her friend must have gone through, the fear, the frustration.

Pastel pulled away from him, putting her head in her hands. She was trembling. "Pam and I begged Ibn to find an alternate way to pay. Said said the agreement was drawn and wouldn't be rescinded. They call it honor." Features contorted, she looked up at him. "Can it be honorable to sell babies to a

lecherous man who would destroy their babyhood
and childhood . . . perhaps ultimately their lives?"

"No, it's foul, wrong under any circumstances."

Pastel wiped her eyes. "Pam decided the only
thing to do was to hide the girls. She believed that if
the girls were safe someplace, she could convince Ibn
not to let the sheikh give them away. She arranged
for the girls' nurse to have a day off and for me to
come to the house. On the pretext of taking the girls
for a walk, I got them out of the house, then went
into hiding with them. Pam and I had arranged to
keep in touch through some friends still working
for the Volunteers. She was to let me know when
it was safe to bring the girls back. I never heard
from her."

He leaned over her, seeking to comfort her. At
the first touch of his mouth on hers, his inten-
tions faded and desire—never far from the surface when he was with her—broke through, firing
him like a rocket. He slanted his mouth over hers,
willing to take her pain and give passion, release
her from the agony of yesterday and chain her to
his side.

For a moment her body was pliant against his,
then she abruptly pulled back. He kept her close to
him, though, rubbing his hands over her waist, her
back, down her sides, seeking to soothe. It hurt to
see her tormented.

"So long ago," she murmured, "but it's like

yesterday." A tremor ran through her. "I shouldn't have talked about it."

He kissed her hair. "I won't let you call it back." Sitting away from her, he asked, "When did all this happen?"

"Ten years ago."

"Ten . . . You've raised Pam's daughters for ten years?"

She nodded. "When four months passed and I hadn't heard from Pam, I knew I had to get out of the country. Ibn's family and the sheikh's people were all looking for us, and I had to get out. I managed to get to the American Embassy, sneaking in at night. I claimed the girls were mine and got passports for them. Then I left the country and came back here. It was difficult to keep them hidden from everyone in the business and any reporters, but I managed."

"Where are they now?"

"In a private school. They've been there for two years."

"So they're safe."

She hesitated, then said yes.

"Do I get to see them?"

"*No!*"

When she would have pulled free, he tightened his hold on her. "Don't."

"I can't endanger them. And if Pam's still alive—"

"Why do you say that?"

Her mouth tightened. She lifted her face to his, shaking her head, a tear slipping down her cheek.

"Oh, please, don't. Darling, I'll help."

"You can't," she whispered, her voice hoarse.

He felt her agony like a sword thrust, her loss like a deep wound. "Damn, damn." He held her closer, running his hands over her back and shoulders.

"I send roses to the chapel of our school once a month, asking them to pray for a special intention. I don't give either of our names." She lifted her head, her eyes drenched in tears. "They pray for her, don't they?"

"Yes. Yes, they do," Will said. "They must."

"I have to believe that."

"Believe it."

A sob burst from her.

"Please, darling, don't cry."

She took a deep breath, forcing back her tears. "You're a good man, Will, but not even you could have helped in our dilemma."

"Keep your hope, Pastel."

"I live on it," she said. "I never told my parents. They thought we were fools for leaving the country. Mother and Dad are hard-rock Americans who disapproved of our altruism from the beginning. I didn't tell Pam's family because she'd never been close to any of them." She shook her head. "I was so afraid of doing or saying the wrong thing."

"So you carried your burden alone."

"It was the least I could do for Pam. She would've done it for me." She reached up and patted his cheek. "You've helped me, Will. Believe that. I didn't think anyone could make the fear fade. You did."

"I'm glad." His body thrummed at her simple caress. He'd never wanted anyone or anything more than he wanted her. "I will do anything I can for you. Just don't expect me to climb out of your life."

She studied him, one finger lifting to trace his jaw and up along his cheekbone. "Maybe I don't want you to go." As if her own words startled her, her eyes widened.

"Can't call that back," he whispered. "I won't let you."

He lowered his mouth to hers, tracing her lips with his tongue, outlining their fullness, more aroused than he'd ever been.

When her arms came up, he braced himself to be pushed away. She caught him around the neck instead.

Pastel felt as though a wellspring of feminine passion and delight was rising in her. She needed to let go of the restraint, the stringent hold she'd kept on her feelings, reactions, emotions for so long. She wanted to be, if only for a time, the woman she defined in her modeling. For once she wanted to be the coquette, an eager participant in flirtation. She'd thought it all frozen to death inside her, but a spark had flickered to life. "Do I appeal to you?" she murmured.

"Oh, you appeal, my lovely. Very much." His grip tightened, the tip of his tongue roving the curve of her ear.

The huskiness in his voice drove her wild. She had such a heady, wondrous sense of safety . . . of danger . . . of joy. She leaned up and bit him gently on the lower lip.

"Are you aware of the danger, at this moment, of heart attack, stroke . . . plain ordinary passing out, Pastel Marx?"

She chuckled. "And you're in jeopardy?"

"On the brink. Risk it anyway."

"I will." She kissed his upper lip, then let her mouth course his cheeks. "I like doing this."

"I can't stand it," Will groaned, pulling her into a tighter hold. He pressed his mouth to hers, welding them in a most passionate embrace. They rocked together in the building force, succumbing to the power that was beyond measure.

In slow motion he pushed up the wool sweater and her turtleneck. His fingers found her satin skin. Heat burst through him. Pastel! She was his personal flame who fed on him, and made him wild and strong. When she sighed into his mouth, he thought his insides would melt.

She leaned back, sliding supine on the couch, pulling him with her.

He leaned over her. "I want you."

"I know."

"Since the moment I saw you on that sound stage." He saw the surprise on her face. "True."

"I believe you." There was an awed shyness to her. "Don't tell me that's Alaskan too."

"Beats me. I just know you poleaxed me . . . and all I gave a damn about was getting to know you."

"And you did . . . over salmon steaks."

"So I did." He bent his head, his mouth moving over her breast, covered by the fine fabric of her bra. He sucked there as though she were naked.

"Will!" He was splitting her apart. She had to be part of him. She needed him.

The phone rang.

Pastel moved as though she'd get up.

"I won't answer it," he said against her skin.

"It might be about the shoot."

"The hell with all of it." But he rolled off the couch, landing with a thump on the floor. Ignoring her laughter, he picked up the phone. "Yeah." He looked up at her, rising enough to kiss her between the breasts.

Disheveled, disoriented, she stared at him.

"Yeah. I have it. She'll be there. Sure. Good night." He cradled the phone and grimaced at her.

"Foiled."

"Yeah." He reached up and pulled her down on top of him.

She squealed.

He nuzzled her.

Neither noticed the approach of the dog, hackles high, teeth bared. The growl started deep in his throat.

Will recognized the sound and pushed himself and Pastel up into a sitting position. "Easy, fella. Easy. I wasn't hurting your lady."

"Good boy," Pastel said. "It's all right."

Tension vibrated among the three.

Slowly, the dog relaxed. Will exhaled and Pastel chuckled.

"Whew," he said. "I'll have to use caution around you. Care to retire to the bedroom?"

She bit her lip. "I should get some sleep. That was an early-call reminder you took, wasn't it?"

He nodded. "Look. Let me kennel Rudy . . . and I'll be back." Getting to his feet before she could protest, he whistled to the dog, who hesitated, then followed him. "Look, big guy. As a cupid, you don't make it. Enjoy the kitchen."

The dog whuffed.

Will groaned. "Now is not the time for a potty walk. "At the dog's soft bark, he ground his teeth, then threw on his down vest. "Come on."

Will cursed Rudy under his breath, then he

started to laugh. "Foiled, she called it. Not just by a phone, but by you. Some pal."

The dog finished his business, then wanted to play.

Will exercised him, then whistled him toward the house.

Inside the kitchen he gave Rudy a biscuit, then ordered him to stay. The dog gave him a sorrowful look, then flopped down on a throw rug. Sighing with relief, Will strode into the great room.

Pastel laughed when she saw him. "Everything taken care of?"

"Yes."

"Good."

He was surprised that she seemed so relaxed. He'd expected her to be uneasy about the intimacy they'd just shared. Yet as she walked toward him, she appeared very calm, very much in control.

"I've realized something this evening," she said when she reached him.

"And what's that?"

"That if happiness comes and it's ignored, that's more than stupid. It's tragic."

"I'll buy that."

"So, Will Nordstrom . . ."

"She put her hand on his arm, and he swallowed hard. "So?"

"I think I'd like to taste a little more of this happiness."

"I suppose you know what you're doing to me."

She pressed her lower body to his. "I have an inkling."

"I thought you might." He couldn't clear the hoarseness from his voice.

"Let's see what else I can do to you." She twined her arms around his neck and pressed her mouth to his.

His arms rose instantly, holding her close, his lips closing over hers as though she were sustenance and he was dying of hunger. His body churned to hardness, eager for her bare flesh, wanting to be buried in her forever. One arm lowered until it caught under her buttocks. He lifted her, not ending the kiss, but deepening it.

Teeth grazed teeth, tongues reached out for each other. There was a terrifying certainty that change, monumental metamorphosis, had just occurred. They could not go back. For all time, the earth had cocked itself into a newer, shinier axis. The firmament glittered their joy. Two people locked together against time, turning the planet with the power, fire, and ferocity of one volcanic kiss. It changed the world forever.

Finally Pastel pulled back.

Will let her slide down his body.

She breathed as though she'd run up Whiteface at a gallop.

His blood slammed through his veins.

"Will Nordstrom."

"That's me."

"I'm not afraid of you."

"I know."

"I want you."

"I want you."

"I need to slow the pace. Is that being hateful?"

"It's not hateful. And I'm a glutton for cold showers." He could wait. There was even a serene satisfaction in it, despite his throbbing arousal.

"Good night," she murmured.

"Good night."

"Oh, God."

He touched her face with tender, stroking fingers. "What?"

"I hurt too."

"I hope so."

She laughed, patted his cheek with a shaking hand. "You know it's wise."

"I know I want you."

"Same here." She stepped around him and sauntered toward the stairs.

Only a careful observer would have noticed the tremor in her limbs.

SIX

"How goes it, Anchor Bliss?"

The voice on the telephone shook him so much, the pencil fell from his fingers. The papers in his other hand fluttered to the floor.

"Have you done it?"

"No," he whispered with despair.

"We weren't kidding. Tomorrow latest, or the old lady gets turned in to the police. And we'll let the papers know too."

"I hear you." Anchor hung up the phone. He couldn't listen to the satisfaction in the hated voice. They'd do it. He put his head down on the desk. Why? Why? Just when life seemed good. His job was everything to him. Most people around him knew that. Damn! No matter what he did, no matter how he handled it or which way he moved, it would be some kind of death. For his mother. Or for Will Nordstrom.

His mother arrested for gambling, publicly humiliated. It would kill her. How had they manipulated her? They'd done something. It wasn't like her to go overboard.

But did Will deserve betrayal after all he'd done?

"Pastel, you're good." Will whirled her around the edge of the outdoor ice rink.

"Don't be so surprised, Nordstrom." Pastel laughed. "Not only Alaskans can ice-skate. I'm a native New Yorker. We have snow."

He grinned at her. "Nah. That can't be. We have all the snow."

She swung at him playfully, just overbalancing. Her skate shot to the left, catching his. She regained her equilibrium, but Will's feet went out from under him. He released her hand rather than take her down, then he crashed to his side, sliding along the ice, his face bumping into some snow alongside the rink.

"Will!"

"I'm all right." He turned to face her, still prone, spitting snow. "You know, before I met you, I was able to skate and ski."

She laughed. "I'm sorry. My fault."

He rolled to a sitting position. "Hey, I live to make you laugh, lady." He meant it. When she burst into fresh laughter, he grinned. She was as unwound as a summer flower. He felt a personal triumph, sweeter than maple syrup . . . just because she laughed at him.

The sound of the assistant director calling his name dragged his attention from her.

"Hey, Will, can you come over here? Gotta glitch."

"I'll be right there." Will rose to his feet. "Stop smirking, Pastel." He kissed her. "Be right back."

"Never mind. The shoot's in half an hour. I'll be right behind you."

He smiled and skated across the rink.

She watched him go, feeling happy, sad, and very mixed up about the future all at once. Sighing, she waltzed slowly around the rink.

As she walked toward the location trailer just over the hill, she couldn't stop thinking about Will. Last night had been the stormiest encounter of her life. Nothing had ever been more sexual, more exciting, and they'd done little more than kiss. She longed for more, needed it, hungered for it. She only hoped she'd feel ready for it soon.

Will saw her walking toward the location and started back to her, intending to meet her halfway. He stopped when he caught a movement to his left. Just a vague shape among the trees, but some instinct told him it was a man. He started running.

Pastel saw him coming and smiled, but the smile

quickly changed to concern when she saw his expression. "Will?"

She didn't have the chance to say any more, for he swept her up in his arms, then rolled with her to the ground.

"Will!"

"Stay down!" He looked up toward the trees and saw a man emerging. He was ready to call over to the crew for help when the man shouted to him.

"Easy, Mr. Nordstrom. It's me, Keen. I saw you running down the hill. Did you see something?"

Will exhaled, recognizing one of Dov's men. He stood and helped Pastel up. "I'm not sure. It was just a movement." He pointed in the direction.

Keen waved his arm. Two men appeared out of the trees. "You can take Ms. Marx to the trailer, Mr. Nordstrom. We'll check the area."

Will nodded.

"What was it?" Pastel asked as they headed for the trailer. "Or who?"

He shook his head. "I'm not sure I saw anyone, or anything. Mostly gut instinct. It could've been deer." He shrugged. "I got scared, so I ran."

"And scooped me up like a forklift."

"Something like that."

"Not a figment of your imagination?"

Her shaky smile had him yanking her into his arms. "Maybe." He kissed her temple, his mouth lingering there. "I don't know. Maybe I'm getting paranoid."

"Fine. I believe in precautions."

They entered the trailer, and Will shut and locked the door. "I meant what I said about taking care of you."

She smiled. "I'm getting the message."

There was a rap on the trailer door. "Pastel? Five minutes."

"Right." She was astonished when Will sat down on the one small chair, overwhelming it.

"I'm not leaving."

She opened her mouth, then closed it. "I don't have time to argue." She picked up her outfit for the shoot and squeezed into the tiny bathroom. "This isn't easy, you know," she shouted through the door.

Will grinned, some of the trepidation fading. "You can dress out here."

"Cretin."

He chuckled, but his eyes were cold as he studied the room. Some instinct told him more was going on with her than she'd told him. Regardless, he'd do anything to keep her safe.

She returned to the main room to check her makeup and hair. "It's unnerving to have someone stare," she said as she adjusted an earring.

"Can't help it. Beauty fascinates me." When she blushed, he smiled.

"Will."

"What?"

"Do you think there was someone after me?"

He hesitated, then shook his head. "I don't know."

"Maybe I already have the answer."

Helpless to prevent the pain he saw building in her eyes, he went to her and pulled her into his arms. "I will protect you."

"You did. Now." She trembled. "I'm still afraid." She licked her lips, gripping his waist. "I need to believe that it will work out." She looked up at him. "So much at stake."

"I know."

She shook her head. "I'm late."

His grip tightened. "I won't let anything or anyone hurt you."

Pastel didn't answer. He didn't know his adversaries. She couldn't allow him to become too involved. He could become a target. The only hope was to wait it out. Will could be hurt if he pushed. She reached up and kissed him.

She meant it only to be a brief kiss, but his arms tightened around her, his lips firm against hers.

She opened her mouth under his, her heart thundering at the chaotic joy that flooded her. Never in her life had she experienced such a rush of longing, such a shattering certainty that her life had changed forever because of one very positive man who was sure he could handle anything.

A knock at the door forced them to stop.

Out of breath, Pastel put both hands against his chest. "Have to go."

"I know."

She opened the door and glanced back at him. "See you."

"Right behind you."

"But don't you have work—"

"Not as important."

Pastel didn't argue. She hurried to her spot and lost herself in the shoot.

Outside, Will saw Keen and motioned to him. "What did you find out?"

"Tracks. A man's by the size, tall and muscular by the depth in the snow. Maybe a sightseer."

Will nodded, but he didn't believe that any more than he suspected Keen did.

"Also tire marks. Looked like a big car. Dov's looking into it."

Will kicked the snow. "I want more people. Something's going on here and I want to know what." He handed Keen a piece of paper with the names of Pastel's friend and her husband and their address in Nahumi. "Get someone on this. Find out everything."

"Yes, sir."

❖━━━━━❖━━━━━❖

Will watched Keen until he disappeared into the woods, then he headed back toward the trailer. He stopped when he saw her leave the shooting area. Pastel had just finished and she walked over to him.

"Aren't you cold?" she asked.

He grinned. "Not after that kiss you just gave him."

She sent him a quelling look. "Well, I'm cold. That director is a perfectionist."

"I'd be glad to warm you, ma'am."

Her eyes widened. "I'll use the trailer, thanks just the same."

He followed her, then opened the door for her. Before he stepped inside the trailer, he looked back over the area. He saw nothing suspicious. Inside, Pastel had taken off her coat, and the sight of her in the sleek white catsuit she was wearing for the shoot sparked his desire. He moved up behind her and slipped his arms around her.

"If you're still cold," he whispered, "we could go back to the chalet and start a fire."

She arched away from him. "You move fast, Nordstrom."

He dropped his arms. "Actually, I'm dragging my heels, though only in deference to the way you feel."

"And how is that?" A reluctant laugh escaped her when he grimaced.

"You're trying to keep me out of your life. I'm trying to get in, stay in, any way I can. We're butting heads . . . but it's getting friendlier."

"Oh, it is, is it?"

"Yes, ma'am. You haven't ordered me out of the chalet—"

"I can't. You leased it."

"That's splitting hairs, and you know it."

"Would you go if I asked?"

"Dragging my steps . . . and I'd get a sleeping bag and camp on the deck."

"Can't have you getting pneumonia."

"I can stay?" He beamed at her, his arm going around her waist, pulling her to his side.

She leaned into him. "I can do just so much fighting."

Will bit back a groan. She was coming closer to him. Maybe he should call Keen back. No! He needed to know who intimidated her. "Then let's share the load. I've got a great right hook."

She chuckled. "So have I."

They faced each other, grinning like two children. Then Will sobered.

"Pastel, tell me the name of the school the girls are in."

She hesitated, then she told him.

Will went to the phone and talked for quite

some time. When he hung up, he turned to her. "Big Mike will drive up to Carlyle himself, check the place out. He'll probably arrange to have one or two people stay on, either in the town or at the school, to keep an eye on the girls."

"Just like that. How can Mike do all this?"

Will shrugged. "Like I told you, he used to work for the State Department. But considering everything Mike knows about security, I think his job involved a lot more than verbal diplomacy."

Pastel smiled, thinking she could say the same thing about Will. She knew she shouldn't feel such relief, such certainty that the girls were somehow safer than they'd been an hour ago. Still, she couldn't fight the flood of good feeling.

"I'll know later just how well we're doing," Will said.

She held out her hands to him, but he'd done no more than grasp them when someone pounded on the trailer door.

"Pastel! Pastel! C'mon. The sun's right. We need you now."

"I'm coming."

She tried to pull free, but Will wouldn't let her.

"What's the matter?" she asked.

"That was Clem. Where's Anchor?"

She shrugged. "He was here earlier."

"I know. But he stays for the whole shoot, oversees the job."

"Maybe he had a problem to solve."

"Maybe."

When the shoot resumed, Will watched Pastel but kept an eye out for Anchor. He didn't appear. Nagged by an unnamed worry, he gestured to the assistant director.

"Clem. Where's Anchor?"

"He left, Will. Said he had things to do back in the city."

Will frowned. "What? Why?" When Clem shook his head, Will pointed to the array of vehicles. "Can I borrow one of the snowmobiles?"

"Sure."

Will chose the biggest machine. He strapped on the helmet, then fired the machine. Snowy wind pelting his face mask and dinging off his helmet, he opened the machine up and sailed over the snow like a land-bound rocket.

Anchor Bliss. Where was he? He didn't leave a location shoot without a word, especially a shoot he'd sweated bullets over. Will ground his teeth. Was he going nuts over this thing with Pastel? Blowing things out of proportion?

He didn't lessen his speed as his mind computed the information and questions he fed it. Why did Anchor have to go back to the city? No explanation. Not like the man. Still, it could have been a sudden emergency, perhaps a family problem. He had a mother who lived upstate, a sister in Vermont.

Will aimed the machine over a four-foot drift, revving it down a natural chute between winter-denuded maples and evergreens, then roared up an icy incline and skidded into a turn above a narrow thoroughfare.

Blood pounding, heart thudding in time to the screeching motor, he wondered what could have happened. Anchor not coming to work was like Congress deciding not to be in session . . . forever. Was he sick? Clem would have noticed and mentioned it. Maybe it was nothing, but it felt like something. And these days, when his sensors were at high frequency, his determination to protect Pastel his greatest priority, he had no intention of ignoring signals from his inner self. Why hadn't Anchor come to him if he had to go back to the city? An acid taste in his mouth, he cranked the throttle.

Opening up until the engine protested, he plunged down a hillside into an area not far from the chalet.

He had too much open road and not enough snow to get right to the motel where the staff was staying. He parked at the chalet and ran for his Bronco. Gunning it into life, he sped down the driveway.

The short drive seemed to take forever.

He reached the motel and looked up to the

second floor balcony, where Anchor's room was. Was he there? As he watched, a door opened and Anchor backed out, suitcase in hand, fumbling for his key.

Will leaped from the Bronco and raced up the outside steps. "Wait! Anchor!"

Anchor paused, key in hand. Then he shook his head. "I quit."

"No, you don't."

"I do."

"Get back in that room."

Anchor swallowed. "You don't understand—"

"Right. And you're going to set me straight."

Anchor backed into the room because Will was pushing on his chest. "They could be watching—"

"Who?"

Anchor sank onto the bed, shaking his head. "Can't tell."

"Yes, you can."

SEVEN

After the shoot was over, Clem drove Pastel back to the chalet. She was surprised to see Will's Bronco was gone. Where was he? She didn't have much time to consider that, for as soon as she walked into the chalet, she was confronted by a gathering of people in the great room. Strangers, all! As she stood motionless by the door, wondering what to do, one man glanced her way and smiled. He started walking toward her, and she realized he was as big as Will. that's when she knew who all these people were. Will's family.

"You must be Pastel," the man said when he reached her. "You're as beautiful as Will said. I'm Lars."

"You're his older brother."

"Guilty."

When he took her hand, Pastel felt a flash of security. Maybe that was Alaskan, too, making people feel safe. Will could do that. Her knees were still knocking with the shock of seeing so many people when she'd unlocked the chalet. "Will said you were coming."

Lars grimaced. "I hope you don't feel overwhelmed. Most of them were supposed to stay home." He shrugged. "They . . . we have a thing about Will. He's never shown such an interest in one . . . that is, he's always liked women a lot . . . mean, it's weird . . ." He shook his head, laughing. "He'll kill me."

Pastel bit her lip, some of her trepidation leaving her. Will had a network of love called family. Some of that warmth penetrated the coldness that had surrounded her for years. She inclined her head to the group. "How many?"

"Oh, no need to worry. We have rooms—"

"But aren't you staying for dinner?" She felt a dart of disappointment.

"I suppose we could. Maybe Will won't like it." He grinned, then turned his head when the laughter rose several decibels. "Too noisy for you?"

"No. I like it." She meant it. It was wild and wonderful. His family, like Will, could chase all the bogeys away. "Did Will say what he wanted for dinner?" Did she still remember how to cook? It'd been a while since she'd tried. Mrs. Dietz, her live-in housekeeper, had been an answer to a prayer, not just because she cleaned, but her cooking was better than average.

"Will? We haven't seen him."

Pastel blinked. "Really? He left the location before me. They said he'd been in an awful hurry. I assumed it was to meet—"

"There he is!" Lars pointed out the window, then touched her arm. "Excuse me, Pastel. I didn't mean to interrupt you."

"That's all right." Pastel walked to the window and looked out. She saw Will and Anchor Bliss getting out of the Bronco. She had no time to wonder what was going on. Will muttered something to his assistant, then bounded up the steps of the chalet and yanked open the door. He saw her immediately and pulled her into his arms, kissing her hard.

Pastel couldn't get her breath, but she couldn't stop kissing him back. From some far-off place she heard hoots and hollers, but she didn't care. She was where she wanted to be.

Will wrenched his mouth from hers. "Are you all right?"

"Yes, but—"

"Good." He took hold of her shoulders and turned her. "Say hello to my mother and father. Lars, come with me."

Pastel felt as though she'd stepped into a hurricane. "Where are you going?" Will was avoiding her! That was strange. "Wait! I want to know."

Will hesitated as everyone in the room turned to look at them.

"It's my fault," Anchor said.

Every head turned toward him.

Will glowered at his assistant. "Chill out—"

"Tell me." Pastel spoke through her teeth.

Will stared at her. "I don't know everything. I'm waiting for a phone call." He shook his head. "It seems you've been followed." When she whitened, seemed to sway, he reached for her.

She put up a hand, keeping him back. "It can't be. Everything is in place . . . except—"

"Except?"

"I'm here."

"That can't be so bad."

It was as though they were alone in the world, apart from the rest of the planet.

"I don't know. I haven't left Manhattan since . . ." She bit her lip.

Will wanted to ask, "Since when," but now wasn't the time. "I'll take care of it," he said.

Her smile was fleeting. "Caretaker to the world."

"To you."

"I don't know. You shouldn't be involved."

He ignored that. "I'll take care of it, I promise," he said, pulling her into his arms. "I won't let anyone hurt you."

"But they told me—" She stopped abruptly.

Will's eyes narrowed. "They? Who are 'they,' Pastel? Has someone from Nahumi contacted you?"

She looked at his family, who were watching them with undisguised curiosity. "Can we talk about this later?" she whispered.

"All right." He gave her a hard look. "But we *will* talk about it, Pastel. I can't protect you and the girls if I don't know everything." He kissed her cheek. "Let me help."

Before she could answer, he went on. "Now, I want to introduce you to my mother and father. They're waiting across the room, probably discussing my poor manners in not bringing you to them at once." He kissed her forehead. "Then we'll talk. I won't keep anything from you." He led her toward an older couple.

Will introduced his parents, Mary and Helborg. Pastel hadn't been talking to them for more than a few minutes when the phone rang. Will strode across the room and snatched up the receiver.

"Nordstrom. Now? Good. Great idea."

When he hung up, they were all staring at him. "That was Mike." He glanced at Anchor. "Some of his friends have taken care of your mother. She's on an extended vacation with her cats. Her house is being watched. And she won't be going back into it until it's safe."

Anchor swallowed, swiping at his eyes. "I

should've trusted you from the start. I won't make that mistake again. What can I do? How can I help?"

"Go on with the shoot," Will said. "There'll be new people all around you . . . helpers who will be running interference, and a group you won't even see. Business as usual."

Helborg stepped forward. "I think we should leave now, get settled into our place. Call, Will, when you figure out what you need me to do to help.

Will clasped his father's hand. "I'll do that."

"You'd better," Lars said. He hugged Pastel. "Welcome to the family." He kissed her on the mouth, then cocked his head at Will, laughing. "Your face is red, brother."

"Lars, you're pushing," Will said through his teeth.

Mary glared at her sons. "Be sensible, Will. Don't let your silliness cloud your judgment. Lars, stop goading your brother."

"Sorry. Mother's right." Lars chuckled. "I couldn't resist."

Helborg scowled at his eldest. "You mustn't tease Will. Though, I must say, it's most interesting to see." He grinned. "He's every bit as bad as Rafe was."

"I think he is." A tall, shapely chestnut-haired woman approached Pastel, reaching past her to poke

Will in the chest. "Neanderthal." She glanced at Pastel, smiling. "I'm Andrea, Will's sister. Everybody calls me Andy."

"How do you do," Pastel said.

Andy laughed. "You have such a ladylike way of handling being overwhelmed."

In a whoosh of movement and laughter, the family and Anchor were gone.

Alone with Will, Pastel moved to the center of the room. Looking at him over her shoulder, she noted his male beauty, his strength. She wanted nothing more than to sink into his arms, forget the world, lose herself in him, let him give her the passion that aroused and cleansed. Fear for him battled the faith that he could do anything. He could be hurt . . . even killed, if he called down her enemy's enmity on himself. Diplomatic immunity still made it easy to get away with crime, even the ultimate one. The man who'd been in touch with her never gave her much information about himself or his cohorts, but he'd assured her they had the protection of the United States government, and that of Nahumi.

She turned to face Will. "Tell me what happened to Anchor."

Will grimaced, then strode to her side. "He was threatened."

"Why?"

"Apparently someone needed a source of information about our shoot here. "They threatened to have his mother arrested for nonpayment of a gambling debt if he didn't cooperate with their demands. Those included what was going on with the shoot, the people involved, a complete dossier on me. Anchor would be able to cover her debts by doing all of this and more—"

"About me." Sighing, she walked away from him and sank down on the couch in front of the fireplace. "It never stops. They know when I breathe."

"I'll take care of it . . . and eradicate the problem."

"Just like that."

"Yes."

"Damn you, Nordstrom, you make me feel safe."

"That's the idea." He sat beside her.

"I can't be that way. Complacency could destroy everything." She looked up at him.

"Tell me what's going on."

"You know most of it."

"But not all."

"They could kill you."

When he laughed, she looked away from him, chin trembling.

His hand on her cheek turned her back to him. "Pastel, I'm not taking this lightly. I just think I can help. I know I can."

She chewed her bottom lip. "I could leave."

He shook his head. "Don't. You're not listening

to me. We can sort this out, settle it. You can't keep running."

"I haven't been running. Cowering, hiding, yes. But not running."

"Let's change that."

"No more hiding?"

"Right."

"Just like that."

"Pretty much." He leaned over her. "We'll handle it together. For now we need to take precautions. You'll stay with my family at their chalet tonight. Lars and I will stay here and—"

She shook her head. "No."

"This isn't a big deal. I just want you as safe as possible while I figure out our next step." His mouth tightened. "We're going on the attack, Pastel."

"This place could be watched—"

"No doubt it is."

"They'll be as cautious as you. Don't think they won't check to see if we're home. They will. If you and Lars are the only ones here, they'll stay away." She swallowed. "You're the one who said no more hiding. Then you turn around and tell me to run and hide. Not good, Nordstrom."

"I'll be better knowing you're safe."

"What makes you think I'll be safe anywhere? Money is behind them, a great deal of it. They have the time and the resources to be thorough. I don't like the idea of confrontation—"

"You don't need to see them—"

"But I'm tired of the game." She looked up at him. "I thought I could protect the girls by being as passive as possible, paying them money—"

"Money? You didn't say anything about that."

Her mouth twisted. "That's the only reason I agreed to do this shoot. I needed the money. Part of my earnings go to pay the school, but most of it pays . . . them, whoever they are."

"How long?"

"Two years."

"Damn! You've been paying blackmailers for two years?"

Her temper flashed. "What did you think I would do? Just hand the girls over to them?"

"No, of course not. That's not what I meant." He gathered her into his arms. "I'm just so damn sorry you've had to deal with this alone for so long."

She allowed herself to relax against him. "I was willing to do anything to keep Althea and Yasmin safe."

"Do they know where the girls are?"

"I'm sure they don't. As soon as they started asking for money, I enrolled the girls in the Carlyle School. It's been tough on them since I can't let them come home for holidays, but I sneak up there whenever I can to visit them."

"I wonder," Will said musingly, "why they haven't tried to force you to give the girls back."

Pastel sat up. "I would think the deal with the prince fell through pretty quick after I took the girls. They may not be worth anything now, except for my money."

"Which they aren't going to get anymore." He turned to face her. "We have to bring them out in the open. That's why I want you out of the way."

She shook her head. "No. They have to see me, think everything is fine."

"You're stubborn, Pastel."

"And I'm tough."

"You are. But still, I'll ask Lars to stay in the garage tonight."

"It isn't heated."

Will chuckled. "Pastel, he won't be cold. We've camped out when it was well below zero. He'd be fine."

"Let him stay in the house."

"He'll be fine in the garage. As for you . . . we're sleeping in the same bedroom."

She stared at him.

"You might have to marry me, Pastel. I'm not very circumspect."

Pastel surprised herself by laughing.

"Don't bet on it."

◆━━━━━━━━━━◆

After dinner Pastel took a shower and ran the astounding day around her head. Was she really going to sleep with a man she scarcely knew? Had meeting Will, after leading a solitary life, put her over the edge? There'd been other men she could have gone to bed with. Will Nordstrom was the first to drive her crazy. It was no one-night stand for her.

She wanted him. Would that desire cloud the solid reasoning that had put her into a semicloistered life originally? Her solid reasoning seemed based on quicksand when she looked at it through Will's eyes.

Hope was a funny commodity. It could put her off balance, remove her prudence. But a trickle of it was turning into a wellspring inside her.

Things had gotten out of hand . . . too complicated. Only one thing seemed crystal-clear. She wanted Will. Lord! What a fool she was. That was the most complex and twisted element of all.

She and Will were in the house alone.

They were ensconced in a large home up behind Lake Placid, guards around them, but virtually alone.

She had the sure sensation that she would cross the Rubicon of her life that night. There was little to know about tomorrow, even about the next minutes or hours. She didn't feel nervous. Serene, in tune, were better descriptions. She'd come to want Will Nordstrom very much. She was sure he felt the same. Tonight she was going to find out just how in sync their feelings were.

She dressed in a cotton nightshirt, then returned to her bedroom. She set out the clothes she'd wear the next day, neat, orderly, and at hand. If she had to leave in a hurry, she could dress in seconds. Next to her things she placed the butcher knife she'd removed from the kitchen. Her weapon.

Lying down in the bed, she picked up a book from the nightstand. She opened it, stared at the introductory pages, the notation about the Library of Congress, and what catalogue number the work would be listed under. That was about all the interest she could muster.

Will Nordstrom was on her mind.

Several minutes passed. Increasingly jumpy, she had half a mind to search him out.

When her door to the bathroom opened, she looked up. "Will."

"Yes." He closed the door behind him, approaching the bed. He looked down at the quilt, at the book she held, then at her. "I don't expect trouble—"

"But there could be. I know."

He inhaled, exhaled, looked around the room, at the windows. "I checked everything again."

"Something else on your mind?" Was he nervous, she wondered. The thought tore through her like a lightning bolt. The burning was more than pleasant, and so was the amusement that accompanied it. *He was nervous.* Wonderful. Her trepidation faded.

He stalked up and down her bedroom a few times.

"Care to sit on the bed?" she asked.

"Yes." He plunked down on the end, staring at her. "It isn't any news to you that I'm attracted to you."

"Correct." She smiled. Attracted to him? Just a tad. A milk-and-water description for a volcanic eruption of passion and sensation. He was a magnet to her metal. And she felt like gold and platinum around him. "And?"

"And . . . I want you to be safe." He looked down at the bed, plucking at the quilt. "Even from me. Always. I want to care for you."

"Big job." And if he was leading up to some sort of celibate sharing of the bed, she'd set him straight!

"Yeah." He studied the coverlet as though he'd memorize the quilting. Then he stiffened, head snapping up, his eyes narrowing. "You're *laughing* at me."

"Not true. I'm doing my damnedest not to."

"Very cute. Your mouth is quivering. You're not doing a good job of holding back. You're laughing at me."

"*With* you."

"I'm not laughing."

"You will be."

"Oh? How so?"

"You tell me what you wanted to say first."

"Pastel, you're very secretive. I understand that. You've taken great pains to hide things from me." He held up his hand when she opened her mouth. "Don't get me wrong. I comprehend the need to protect, even hiding out." He frowned. "Though I'm not good at it, I'm trying not to probe, not to crowd. But why the hell did you pick such a visible profession if you wanted to go into hiding?"

She reached into the drawer of the nightstand and pulled out a wallet of photographs. She took one out and handed it to him.

"Who is it?" he asked.

"Me."

He frowned down at the photo, shaking his head. "No."

"Yes."

"Hard to believe."

"That's why it was a good cover."

"How did you lose so much weight?"

"I was always a good size—grade school, high

school, college. I was in sports, so some of it was muscle." She smiled. "Actually I liked the way I looked then. I wanted to be tough, independent, unafraid . . . unfeminine."

Will studied the photo. The girl she'd been was not unattractive, but the extra weight blurred Pastel's distinctive facial features. Something in the way the girl carried herself also seemed to reinforce the sense of plainness, as though she didn't consider herself pretty and didn't expect anyone else to.

"There's some resemblances," he said, "but you'd have to be looking for it."

She shrugged. "I don't think there's any likeness."

"It's pretty amazing that added weight could change a person's appearance that much."

"Not always. In my case it did."

She paused. "That's the way I looked in Africa most of the time I was there. Then I went into hiding with the girls. Trying to survive with little money, less food, and almost no access to help can strip off excess fat and muscle faster than I realized. One day I looked in the mirror and didn't recognize the person. Then I knew I had a chance. Since I hadn't heard from Pam, I felt I had to get back to the States. By then I was pretty thin."

"How long were you in hiding?"

"Quite a while."

"Weeks . . . months . . . ?"

Get swept away...

Enter the

Winner's Classic Sweepstakes

and discover that love has its own rewards.

You could win a romantic 14-day rendezvous for two in diamond-blue Hawaii...the gothic splendor of Europe...or the sun-drenched Caribbean. To enter, make your choice with one of these tickets. If you win, you'll be swept away to your destination with $5,000 cash!

or take $25,000 Cash!

Get 4 FREE Loveswept Romances!

 Whisk me to Hawaii

 Carry Me Off To Europe

 Take me to the Caribbean

 Pamper me with FREE GIFTS!

GET A FREE GIFT!

Get this personal, lighted makeup case. It's yours absolutely FREE!

NO OBLIGATION TO BUY.
See details inside...

Get Swept Away To Your Romantic Holiday!

Imagine being wrapped in the embrace of your lover's arms, watching glorious Hawaiian rainbows born only for you. Imagine strolling through the gothic haunts of romantic London. Imagine being drenched in the sun-soaked beauty of the Caribbean. If you crave such journeys then enter now to...

WIN YOUR ROMANTIC RENDEZVOUS PLUS $5,000 CASH!
Or Take $25,000 CASH!

Seize the moment and enter to win one of these exotic 14-day rendezvous for two, plus $5,000.00 CASH! To enter affix the destination ticket of your choice to the Official Entry Form and drop it in the mail. It costs you absolutely nothing to enter—not even postage! So take a chance on romance and enter today!

Loveswept®

Has More In Store For You With
4 FREE BOOKS and a FREE GIFT!

We've got four FREE Loveswept Romances and a FREE Lighted Makeup Case ready to send you!

Place the FREE GIFTS ticket on your Entry Form, and your first shipment of Loveswept Romances is yours absolutely FREE—*and that means no shipping and handling.*

Plus, about once a month, you'll get four *new* books hot off the presses, *before they're in the bookstores.* You'll always have 15 days to decide whether to keep any shipment, for our low regular price, currently just $11.95.* **You are never obligated to keep any shipment**, and you may cancel at any time by writing "cancel" across our invoice and returning the shipment to us, at our expense. There's **no risk** and **no obligation** to buy, *ever.*

It's a pretty seductive offer, we've made even more attractive with the **Lighted Makeup Case—yours absolutely FREE!** It has an elegant tortoise-shell finish, an assortment of brushes for eye shadow, blush and lip color. And with the lighted makeup mirror *you* can make sure he'll always see the passion in your eyes!

BOTH GIFTS ARE ABSOLUTELY FREE AND ARE YOURS TO KEEP FOREVER no matter what you decide about future shipments! So come on! You risk nothing at all—and you stand to gain a world of sizzling romance, exciting prizes...and FREE GIFTS!

*(plus shipping & handling, and sales tax in NY and Canada)

ENTER NOW TO WIN A ROMANTIC RENDEZVOUS FOR TWO

Plus $5,000 CASH!

or take $25,000 Cash!

No risk and no obligation to buy, anything, *ever!*

Winners Classic

SWEEPSTAKES
OFFICIAL ENTRY FORM

☐ **YES!** Enter me in the sweepstakes! I've affixed the destination ticket for the Romantic Rendezvous of my choice to this Entry Form. I've also affixed the FREE GIFTS ticket. So please, send me my 4 FREE BOOKS and FREE Lighted Makeup Case.

Affix Destination Ticket of Your Choice Here	TICKET	Affix FREE GIFTS Ticket Here	🎁

PLEASE PRINT CLEARLY   CK123   12237

NAME

ADDRESS

CITY   APT. #

STATE   ZIP

There is no purchase necessary to enter the sweepstakes. To enter without taking advantage of the risk-free offer, return the entry form with only the romantic rendezvous ticket affixed. To be eligible, sweepstakes entries must be received by the deadline found in the accompanying rules at the back of the book. There is no obligation to buy when you send for your free books and free lighted makeup case. You may preview each new shipment for 15 days free. If you decide against it, simply return the shipment within 15 days and owe nothing. If you keep them, pay our low regular price, currently just $2.99 each book —a savings of $.50 per book off the cover price (plus shipping & handling, and sales tax in NY and Canada.)

Prices subject to change. Orders subject to approval. See complete sweepstakes rules at the back of the book.

DETACH CAREFULLY AND MAIL TODAY

Don't miss your chance to win a romantic rendezvous for two and get 4 FREE BOOKS and a FREE Lighted Makeup Case!

You risk nothing—so enter now!

"Four months."

He felt the fear she must have known then. "It must've been hell."

His hoarse voice brought her up short. She almost smiled. "Somehow it didn't seem so bad at the time, because my mission was so strong. That sounds corny, I know—"

"I understand."

She knew he did. The comfort, caring, sharing that came off him was like a soft blanket that she needed, and hadn't even known how much. "Funny. You do things you must. When you look back on them, you can be more objective. If someone had laid out my future for me, I would've balked, said 'no way—' "

"But when you had to save yourself . . . and others . . ."

She nodded, her smile watery.

He kissed her hair. "I like being in bed with you. It's arousing, and friendly too."

She nodded. Even recalling those scary days hadn't dimmed her need for him. "But you look like you have more questions in mind."

"You called yourself Pat when you talked about your friend Pam. Pastel isn't your real name. Is Marx?"

She hunched down in her pillows. "I was christened Patricia Stephany Louise Marx Donnelly. What a mouthful. My mother's idea. My maternal grandmother's name was Louise Marx. My paternal grandmother's name was Stephany Donnelly. Mother wanted everyone included. She called me Pastel as a summary for the names. When I left Nahumi, I decided to use the name Marx."

"I understand."

She reached up and curled a hand around his neck, pulling him so close, their lips almost touched. "I hope you understand this." She kissed him, mouth open, welcoming his tongue.

The phone rang.

She pushed back from him, her breathing ragged, speech impossible.

Will groaned. "I can't believe it." He reached for it on the fourth ring.

Pastel stayed his hand. "Let me. If it's the wrong people, at least they'll know I'm home."

Will stiffened. Anger coursed his features, then he nodded. "Answer."

"Hello. Oh, Mrs. Nordstrom. How are you? Yes, I'm fine." Pastel swallowed a laugh when Will fell back on the bed, moaning. "That sound? Just the wind, I think. No wind where you are? Strange, isn't it?"

Will waited, then reached for the phone. "Good night, Mother. See you in the morning." He cradled the phone.

"You were very impolite, Will Nordstrom."

"I was polite." He reared up off the bed and

strode to the bathroom. "She was laughing," he said over his shoulder.

Pastel ached. She wanted him. She reached over and turned out the light.

EIGHT

When Will reentered the bedroom, it was dark.

He tiptoed to the bed and slid in beside Pastel, reconciling himself to a sleepless night. Except for making love to her, which he needed and wanted, he wouldn't have changed anything. Being that near her was heaven. He closed his eyes.

They snapped open when he felt the feathery touch on his thigh.

"Pajamas?" she murmured. "I'll bet you don't always wear them."

"Never do," he managed to say in a throat gone dry. "Good night, Pastel."

"Not tired. Are you?"

"Yes." Desperation made his voice rusty.

Turning over, Pastel stared at him through the gloom, feeling reckless. "Do you have a girlfriend, Nordstrom?"

Will slanted a glance her way. "If I had, do you think I would've been pursing you?"

She shrugged. "Beats me. I don't know you well enough to make—"

"You know me damn well . . . and you also know I've been after you."

Pastel was having a good time. "Touchy."

"Damn touchy. I don't usually share a bed with a woman and chitchat."

"Aren't you open to new experiences?" She tried to ignore the dart of jealousy as pictures of him with other women in other beds floated past her inner vision.

"Very amusing."

"Nordstrom, you don't have a sense of humor."

"I do. Your timing is bad."

"Hormones giving you trouble?"

"You're sadistic to mention it."

"Not me. It's just such a golden opportunity. How could I resist?"

"Shucks, ma'am, I don't know."

"Sarcasm? Shame on you." She touched his lips. "Are your teeth welded together?"

"Almost."

"You should relax. Stress can kill."

"Or drive me crazy."

"I've never heard that one."

He groaned. "Aren't you ashamed of your lack of compassion?"

"Uh-uh."

"I've never seen this side of you. Do you pull the wings off flies?"

"Never touch the things." She leaned over him, placing her mouth on his.

Groaning, Will pulled her to his chest, not releasing her mouth, his hands going over her in urgent, gentle quest.

Pastel caught her breath, then she breathed into his mouth, taking his air, giving hers. "Will."

"Pastel." He turned her on her back, his mouth coursing over her, his hands never ceasing their loving touch. "You're so beautiful," he said against her lips. "I want you so much. I thought you'd decided against it. You're so lovely."

"So are you." When he laughed against her mouth, she pulled back a fraction. "How can you laugh and be so aroused?"

"Practice. I've been aroused since we met."

"Ooo, you must be sore."

"Damned straight."

He lifted his head. "But we have to wait a minute."

She smoothed his tousled hair. "What does that mean?"

"It means I want to make love to you. No. I'm desperate to make love to you. But I won't if it—I mean, I want you to be protected . . . to want it as much—"

"I do."

"You do?" Will's arm fell away from her. He caught himself before he collapsed on her.

She frowned. "Who do you think was just coming on to you? Cinderella?"

"No . . . yes . . . I knew that . . . but I thought you might be teasing—"

"You think I'm a tease?"

"No!"

"Then what?"

"You've been elusive as hell. That's your reputation. I've seen it myself." He shook his head. "I'm not saying this well."

"No, and I'm cooling fast."

He groaned. "Please, don't."

She chuckled, pushing at him.

Aroused, supercharged, but weak as a kitten, he almost fell out of bed when he tried to balance himself. "I want you so much."

"I feel the same."

"You do?"

"Yes." She touched his mouth with her own. "Very much." There'd be time for regrets . . . goodbyes . . . later. There had to be a time to live, to savor passion, to revel in hot emotion.

"Why?" He was a fool to ask.

"Because today, when I saw your family, their fondness for one another, their intensity, I realized how precious life is, how much it belongs to the living. I won't hide behind barricades, real or imagined, anymore. I'm—I'm coming out swinging. I'll protect my girls . . . and myself."

"I'll do that."

"Thank you. I need your help."

"I love you."

His simple declaration almost pushed her from the bed. Daunted at the flood of passion and feeling in his eyes, she recoiled, then clasped him. She couldn't doubt such simple words so plainly spoken. Truth was one syllable. There never was such beauty. She sank down on him. "Your move, Nordstrom."

There was a tremor in his answering laugh. "Will?"

"I'm here." His mouth covered hers with practiced, insistent skill, his hands going over her as though he'd map every pore, indentation, and bone. He'd wanted her for a lifetime . . . for all time. She was in his arms.

Pastel closed her eyes and let the wonderful hypnosis of emotion take her away, bandage the hurts that had clotted her sensations for too long. It was more than surcease from pain. It was taking life in a new dimension, routing a new way of living. She was sure she'd be shy, awkward in the face of his unerring masculinity, the inborn expertise that came from being a true feminist man, in tune with women, in sync with their needs and wants. Instead, she felt eagerness, a joy that was trying to burst through her and flood him.

First he led with his mouth and hands.

Then, as she caught fire and began a tentative exploration of her own, he gave her full access, the reins, the power, of charting the love course.

His mouth and hands enticed her, teased, titillated, and enjoined her to go with him to the land of lovers. His tongue slid over her lips, touching, opening them. Entering in sweet languor, he swept the inside of her mouth, his hands sliding over her breasts and under, squeezing, cupping the nipples.

When she gasped, he lifted back. "Pastel?"

"I'm . . . excited."

"So am I." His mouth became more demanding. There was no going back for him, not since the first meeting. He had every intention of showing her just how much she meant to him. He'd burst through a new curtain of living with her. There was no more Will Nordstrom as an entity. He was Will, part of Pastel. She had to feel that. He needed her to know.

His mouth became more demanding, lingering on her lips, coursing her cheeks, making slow forays over her neck, his teeth nipping at her ears.

When she moaned, his heart raced. He exulted in holding her. It'd been forever . . . and he'd needed her that long.

He let his hands follow his mouth, and they hovered under her breasts, his thumbs flicking over the velvet skin, the pebble-hard nipples. Just when Pastel thought her bones would crack with need, that all the blood would leave her body, he moved his mouth, letting his tongue drive into hers.

A cry filled the room. Pastel didn't realize at first it was hers, that her body had surged to his. Desire was a roaring fire that thundered through her veins. She couldn't get enough of him. A part of her was appalled at the unleashed, unrestrained passion that had burst between them. Her errant thought that she could want Will Nordstrom and be prepared to leave him at some future time had a bizarre ring to it, more than a little touched with unreality.

He tore his mouth from hers. She moaned in protest. When his mouth closed over her nipple, the moan turned to gasping pleasure. She knew she called out his name, but there was no sound. Her throat couldn't muster any.

His hand sliding over her stomach made her tremble. Her limbs, shaking as though they were in the grip of a terrible fever, tried to tighten on him. When he touched the hot triangle between her legs, she cried out again.

At that instant she gave over to him, not just her body, but the spirit of love inherent in a woman that stays caged until the joining is one of indefinable wonder. Should she tell Will she was his? Or would he know?

She muttered her love, though there was no sound. Deep in her heart she committed to him. Lost in dark, silent wanting, she made a vow to Will Nordstrom. She couldn't have called it back had she wished. But could she ever tell him?

Will knew the moment they were one, that their joining was imminent. His desire had become hers; she'd crossed over into molten passion.

Tension left her, her knees fell apart, a poignant giving that made his heart beat a wild tattoo in his chest.

When she attempted to pull him up to her, he resisted. "Darling, I'm loving you," he murmured.

"I know . . . but you should be up here."

"I will be." He let his mouth slide down her body, not hurrying, though he could feel her urgency. The wonderful search was sending his libido past the danger point, but he forced it down. He would love her. She'd forget that anything in her life could hurt and confuse her. She'd know how committed he was to her.

His mouth entered the wonderful cavity. Her body jerked and she keened like a wild thing. Instinct told him that no one had loved her thus. It humbled him, made him a superman.

"Will!"

"I'm here." The huskiness of his voice made it almost unintelligible.

He wanted to devour her with hands and mouth. The more she writhed, the hotter he became; the more entangled their bodies, the more heat was engendered.

"Willll!"

He answered her cry by moving up her body, bracing his weight on his arms, and easing into her slowly.

When she surged against him, it was his turn to groan.

For a moment she was so tight, he thought she might still be a virgin. He hesitated.

"No!" She grasped his head and pulled him to her.

For the first time in his life, Will lost it. He felt torn to shreds, then reassembled in a different way. He'd become another man . . . and yet, never had he felt so sure of who he was and why he lived.

In the most volcanic moment of his life, she took him, and he went with her over the edge into the molten world of rapture that only lovers find. Not the facile fix of a rapid coupling, but a joining of bodies and minds and souls so rampant with passion that nothing could separate them; so flaming joyous that they couldn't have described it if given a library of words. Instead, they lived it.

Limbs entwined, hearts thundering, shaking with reaction, their orgasms came in cascades of beauty that welded them, kept them safe, heated, and cooled them.

Palpitations subsided in slow cadence. Breathing evened.

Eyes turned to each other.

"I didn't know, Will."

"Neither did I, darling."

She grinned. "You've made love to thousands of women."

"Not thousands, and never like that." He turned on his side, enveloping her in his arms. "You're the most beautiful happening in my life, Pastel."

She started to answer, but yawned instead. Feeling more safe, wanted, and content than ever before, she fell asleep.

Morning came through the window in shafts of sun so bright, they stung the eyes.

"Wake up," Will whispered to Pastel.

"Can't." She knew she should move, but it was too wonderful being in his arms.

"Want to shower with me?"

Her stomach dropped to her feet. "Sure," she said, her voice husky.

They rose slowly. She knew he watched her. Her body preened beneath his hot gaze. Shame on you, she told her insides. They paid no attention. "You're staring."

"So are you." He reached out his hand. When she took it, his being trembled. "I feel like I'm flying, not walking." He paused outside the bathroom door. "If this is a dream, Pastel, don't leave a morning call, please." Her laughter made him smile. "I waited all my life for last night . . . and now."

"I enjoyed it too."

He leaned over her, kissing her. "Good."

Showering together was a wonderful closeness. Steamy. The water coursing over them. Their kisses grew hotter. There was nothing between them but skin.

Rubbing against her hardened him. "Sorry, love."

"Don't be." She reached up and clung to him. Will was so shaken, he stepped to one side.

The fragrant soap he'd been using slid under his foot. He reached down to get it, but slipped instead. Feeling himself go, he tried to protect Pastel, get her out of the way. His foot caught hers.

"Oh!"

"Pastel!"

He seemed to fall in slow motion, sliding down the tiles.

Pastel tumbled on top of him.

Tangled with her, soap in his eyes, splayed in the tub, he could open only one eye. "Are you hurt?"

Pastel couldn't stop laughing. "Gosh, what a romantic encounter. I was swept off my feet."

"Very funny."

"It is." She went into gales of laughter, falling forward on his chest. "You're a wild man on the love train, Nordstrom."

"If you think this is cooling me off, Miss Marx, think again."

She looked at him through the wet tendrils of hair strewing her face. "Hot as a firecracker, are we?"

"Yes." Laughter burst from him. "And I don't know how the hell you manage to make lovemaking the most hilarious event in the world."

"Me? I'm not the one doing aerobics in the tub."

He sat up and yanked her onto his lap. "You're beautiful."

She lifted a finger and touched his nose. "So are you."

He kissed her, letting his tongue delve deep. When hers jousted with his, he wondered how quickly he could get her back into bed.

Ringgggg!

Will took no notice.

Pastel pushed back from him. "Phone."

"No," he muttered.

"Might be about the shoot . . . or Mike."

"Right, right." He nodded once. "I'll get it. You finish your—"

The banging at the bathroom door had them struggling erect.

"Yeah!" Will called.

"Will!" Lars answered. "Anchor Bliss is on the phone. Said the conditions are perfect for shooting. What should I tell him?"

"Tell him to go straight to—" Will said.

"Tell him I'll be right there," Pastel said.

Silence, then they heard Lars laughing. "Okay," he said.

"Leave, older brother. Or I'll come through the door after you."

"I'm going."

They could hear his laughter all the way down the stairs.

Will glared at Pastel. "That tears it. I'm going to kill him." He glowered at her for a full minute, then he grinned. "Your reputation's ruined. You'll have to marry me."

Pastel eyed him as she tried to free herself. "Were you propelled backward in your time machine? This is the twentieth, almost the twenty-first, century. Women are able to make choices. To bed or not to bed is not just a male prerogative."

Will looked glum. "Well, then you'd better marry me to save *my* reputation."

"You don't have one."

"I'll tell my mother."

"You're a nut."

"She'll make you marry me. Make an honest man of me."

"Wonderful."

"I thought you'd agree."

Pastel giggled, surprising herself. She'd not had so much fun in a long time. Will had opened a door to a new world for her. His kindness had made her grow, bloom, expand in a short time. She had a new confidence that all would be well. She hadn't cast off all the fear. She might never. But there was a zest to living that hadn't been there before she'd met Will.

She kissed his cheek. "Showering with you has been a blast, but I've got to get ready."

He watched appreciatively as she stepped out of the tub and began drying her body. "If you're going to leave now, maybe I should stay here and take another shower." When she looked questioningly at him, he added, "A cold one."

She laughed.

The shoot went well, without a hitch.

"I still can't believe it's all right," Anchor murmured to Will. "My mother is thrilled with her place. You saved us."

"Turnabout's fair play. You tried to save us, Anchor. I won't forget that."

"I suppose you won't, since I'll be moving into your place in Manhattan."

Will laughed. "I'm used to crowds."

"You'd better be. It'll be damned crowded, if your brother—"

"And father. My other brother and brother-in-law might show up too."

Anchor's mouth dropped. "You're kidding. We'll be tripping over ourselves."

"Maybe. I've leased a town house. Big enough to lose ourselves in, so don't worry, my friend."

Anchor was silent for a moment. "They'll come at you again, Will. Whatever Pastel has, they want it . . . and they don't like being thwarted."

"They won't get it."

The steely certainty almost made Anchor shiver. "I'm with you."

"I knew that."

"Can we win?"

Will nodded. "We have to."

The drive back to Manhattan was even more fun for Pastel than the ride to Lake Placid. She was filled with exuberance and confidence.

"Anchor said the shoot was great. We should've stayed on a few days and celebrated."

Will smiled at her. This was the woman who'd feared to come to Lake Placid. Now she looked over her shoulder with regret. That pleased him, but he had no intention of remaining a minute longer than necessary. In New York she'd be covered better, and by more people.

He glanced at her, not taking his eyes off the road for long. The two-lane highway had a stream of cars coming and going through the huge park. Six million square miles of park could hold quite a few people. The people dogging Pastel could be anywhere.

"You just weaved across the double line, Nordstrom. Want me to drive? I'm better at it."

"Thanks," he said, making a face at her.

"We've kidded around with each other with your family, with Anchor," she said.

"Right."

"But let's not skate around it anymore. What's the game plan for the Big Apple?"

"You're living with me now. I've rented a town house and—"

"I can't."

"Why?"

She was silent for moments. "Will, I—I think Pam's alive."

He jerked his head toward her. "What?"

"When I was first approached two years ago, the guy showed me a letter from her. It was her writing and dated not two days earlier. What I do not only affects the girls. It could also be the difference between life and death for Pam."

Will's breath whushed out of him. "I knew there was something."

"That's it."

"All right. We change the plan, not basically, just on the surface. You stay at your place . . . ostensibly alone. I'll be living there too. The town house I've leased is just down the block from yours. Lars, Anchor, and maybe my father will be staying there."

Pastel didn't answer. She was thrilled Will would be with her, but she wished the circumstances were very different.

NINE

Less than two weeks after their return to Manhattan, Pastel's life had settled into a routine she could happily get used to. Will had moved into her brownstone, and even though she knew he was doing it because he wanted to protect her, she loved sharing her home with him. They were both morning people and would rise early so they could have a leisurely breakfast together. Then Will drove her to her agency—always a wild and crazy ride, since Will seemed to believe he had to outdrive all of New York's notoriously reckless cabdrivers. Sometimes they met for lunch, but usually they just rendez-voused back at her place. Some evenings they joined Lars and Helborg for dinner, some evenings they went out. Pastel preferred the nights they stayed home, making a simple dinner, then watching an old movie on TV or playing Scrabble. Then they would walk to her bedroom arm in arm, and make love. Splendid, delicious, life-changing love.

On Tuesday, Pastel finished early at the agency. Knowing Will had an important meeting that afternoon, she took a cab home. But the house was too empty without him, and on impulse she called him. His secretary said he was still in his meeting, but that she would be sure to leave a note for Will that she'd called. Pastel hung up, frowning.

Rattling around the empty house was unappealing. She didn't feel like reading. The housekeeper had done the chores. Antsy, she ran every conceivable distraction around her brain. Nothing. What she needed was a workout to take off the rough edges. Why not?

Because Will didn't want her doing anything on her own. She bit her lip. It was crazy to run around the house like an idiot when she could work off the head of steam building in her.

What could it hurt? She wouldn't be gone long. She left a note on the hall table and ran to get her gym bag. The Downtown Athletic Club was a short cab ride away. Ordinarily, on such a sunny March day she'd walk. As a concession to Will's concern, she'd take a cab.

Maybe on the return trip she'd stop at Will's town house and visit with Lars and Helborg. They were nice people, and she liked them. They made her feel comfortable, relaxed.

She left the house, hailing a passing cab. "Downtown Athletic Club, please."

"Right."

Intent on checking her bag to make sure she had what she needed, she paid little attention to the driver or her surroundings. The trip was familiar, since she made it three or four times a week.

She looked up when the cab stopped in front of the club. As she was slipping across the seat and handing the driver the money, she noticed he was frowning out the back window. "Something wrong?"

"Naw. I thought we was being followed. My ex is always pulling tricks . . . she thinks I'm loaded." When Pastel twisted around to look back, he took the money and patted her hand at the same time. "Hey, lady, don't get upset. My ex's a bitch, but she doesn't usually battle me in public. She's just nosy."

"Right. Keep the change."

"Thanks."

Pastel didn't pause on the sidewalk. She sprinted for the door under the canvas marquee and entered the club at a jog. Slipping around to the tall window at the front, she positioned herself to one side, almost hidden by the heavy drapes. Gazing up and down the street, she fixed on every passerby, every vehicle. She waited several minutes, but saw nothing unusual, just vendors, pedestrians, autos, and cabs.

Not totally reassured, she turned, catching the mystified glance of the woman at the desk. "Hello, Mil. Thought a friend was going to join me." Her hand shook when she fumbled for her membership card.

"Oh. Here, let me run your card."

"Sure." Pastel watched, glassy-eyed, then took it back with limp fingers. She had to stop imagining things. Will was right. She had to change her perspective. Don't be on the defensive. Change to offensive. Prepare to attack. She could do that.

"Are you all right?" the clerk asked.

"Yes. I guess I really need my workout today."

Mil smiled, nodding. "That's the truth. I can't function without it now."

"Up and at 'em. That's my new mantra."

"Right."

Just saying it out loud gave her a surge of confidence. Why shouldn't she be on the offensive? She'd done nothing. Trying to protect children wasn't a crime. The criminals were the ones who'd threatened the girls. Bolstered, she marched through the door marked WOMEN.

Stripping down in front of her locker, she vowed to cringe no longer. She was ready for a fight . . . as long as she had Will. Smiling to herself, she changed into her bathing suit, grabbed her cap, goggles, and earplugs, and walked through to the shower room. After rinsing off, she entered the pool area. Empty! She couldn't believe her luck. She glanced at the lifeguard, who grinned, knowing what she was thinking. Swimming by herself was a luxury she'd never before enjoyed at the busy athletic club.

Stepping to the foot of the pool, she jumped in, as was the rule. No diving at lap time. Too dangerous. She slipped into a comfortable crawl that took her up and down the twenty-five-meter pool easily. The silky, smooth water began its work.

Her jumbled thoughts settled, tension eased out of her limbs. Disjointed future plans melded to a simple plan.

Her stroke increased in speed until she was swimming up and down the pool at near-competitive speed. Swimming was her tranquilizer, her buffer against stress, her comfort against the bogeys. Blood thundered through her, adrenaline surging. All that had seemed insurmountable began to have solutions.

She finished at a sprint, out of breath, and feeling greatly loosened up and revived. She did two cool-down laps, then stopped, sighing, at peace, her eyes closed.

Climbing out of the pool, she waved to the guard and entered the shower room. Cooling off with a quick cold sluicing, she left the area and walked down the long hallway to the common steam room. It was larger and easier to control than the one in the women's locker room. Checking the thermometer, she opened the wooden door. There was another person at the other end of the room. Pastel didn't speak. She wasn't sure if the other occupant was a man or woman because of the towels draped over the person's head, shoulders, and body.

When the other person rose, going to the thermometer inside the unit, Pastel barely noticed. She intended to stay for only a few minutes, so she didn't care if the temperature went higher or lower. Then the person walked past her, heading for the door that led to the women's locker room. Must be a woman, Pastel thought, but she needed to shave her legs.

Pastel sat back and tried to relax, but quickly became uncomfortable. The steam was rising in choking clouds. Did the fool, whoever she was, forget to turn it down when she went outside? "Forget this," she muttered. She wasn't going to bother with the interior thermometer. It was across the room. She couldn't see for the puffing steam. She'd take care of it outside. Then, if she found the woman in the locker room, she'd point out a few things to her.

Coughing, she grabbed her towel, feeling her way to the door.

She pushed. Nothing. Again. She threw her shoulder against it. Stuck. Damn. She couldn't budge it. Sweating, out of breath, and feeling suffocated, she called out. "Hey! Anybody out there? Somebody? Could you help me with this door?"

Exhausted, she leaned against the door. She had to get out of there. The choking heat was making her dizzy.

She'd cross the room and go out the men's side. As she was turning, she felt a movement. She couldn't see, but she knew someone was there beside her. "Hey!" When a hand circled her neck, she tried to scream, but no sound went past that locked hold.

"You don't learn, Pastel Marx. We mean what we say. You get rid of those hangers-on that are dogging you, or we will. Especially Nordstrom. Cross us and the girls suffer." The grip tightened for an instant, then she was free.

"Stop!" A door slammed.

Pastel tried to run. She stumbled over something, fell to the floor. Fighting for breath, reeling, panic rising like a flood in her, she struggled onto her hands and knees. Better to crawl. She couldn't stop coughing. Her throat hurt like hell. She had to get out! But which way?

Suddenly the door to the women's lockers was pushed open. It hit her in the side.

"Oh. I'm sorry. Are you all right? Here, let me help you." The woman put a hand under her arm. "Gosh, it's really hot in here. Too hot for me."

Pastel's first instinct was to pull away, but reason told her this wasn't her assailant. "Thank you. I suppose I stayed in too long."

"Oh, my. Mustn't do that. You should read the instructions beside the door."

"I'll do that."

"You sure you're all right?"

"Yes. Thank you very much." She stumbled out of the steam room, gulping cool air into her lungs, feeling burned from the toes up.

The woman stared at her, frowning. "Shall I get some help for you?"

"No, no, I'm all right. I'll just lower the temperature." Hands shaking, she squinted at the reading. Lord, she could've boiled in there. "Thanks."

"You're welcome." The woman checked the thermometer again, then entered the steam room.

Pastel stared at the closed door and shuddered.

Fright had her looking up and down the hallway, peering around the door before she entered the locker room. A group of women entered the shower area, and she scrutinized each face. They ignored her, absorbed in their conversation.

Trembling from head to foot, she showered, dried off, and dressed in her underwear, all in record time. Alone in the dressing room, she looked into the mirror. Seeing her white face, the scared look, she started to cry. Big hulking sobs shook her, but she couldn't have stopped it if she tried. She didn't, sensing the need for release.

Finally her crying eased and stopped. She

pressed a towel to her face and went to the sinks, dousing her face with cold water.

Several minutes later, still shaking, she donned her makeup. After all but jumping into her clothes, she grabbed her bag and opened the door leading to the lobby. Pausing, she looked left and right and up to the glass-walled second floor. No one.

A few members hailed her. She smiled, not pausing.

She left the building, staying under the marquee until a cab pulled to the curb. She huddled down in one corner, concentrating on not screaming.

"Pastel! Where are you?" Will was excited. He'd rushed home from the office a little early, ignoring the sheaf of messages his secretary had shoved into his hand. He wanted to tell Pastel the good news. The first editing had been done that day on the Lake Placid shoot. It'd been a difficult job, because so much of it was good. Some was already in the hopper for initial advertising that would presage the big push in the fall. That would escalate into the Christmas advertising.

He'd called Pastel's agency before he left his office and had been more than irked when he'd found out she had left for the day. He'd hung up before her secretary could finish her message. Something about free time. Why the hell hadn't she phoned?

"Pastel?" he called again.

A woman appeared from the back of the brownstone. "Can I help you, sir?"

"Who are you?" Will asked, instantly on the alert. "Where's Miss Marx?"

"I'm Wilhelmina de Roos. I'm replacing the regular housekeeper, who's down with the flu. Who are you?"

"Will Nordstrom " he snapped. "Pastel!"

"No need to bellow. She ain't here. Went to the gym. Read the note she left you." She fumbled in her apron pocket.

"What?" Angry, he snatched the proffered paper. He read it, then looked up, grinding his teeth. "Why didn't you stop her?"

"I ain't no bouncer. I'm hired to cook and clean. Call me if you want tea. Use that infernal speaking machine if you must. But don't expect me to answer. Can't abide 'em." Wheeling away, she stalked back to the kitchen, her gait resembling that of a lumbering buffalo.

Will stared after her, caught between having her checked out at once or going after Pastel. Grabbing his briefcase, he pawed through it until he found the notes his secretary had given him. Rifling through them, he found the one from Pastel. Damn!

He was mulling his next move when the door opened behind him. He turned, catching sight of Pastel. He opened his mouth to blister her hide for not waiting for him, but he was stopped by her stricken look, her pallid hue.

She didn't notice him as she slipped into the house, almost like a thief. Puzzled, he inhaled some calming breaths and waited.

She stood at the narrow window beside the door, inching aside the sheer curtain that hung there. Several minutes passed. She didn't budge.

"What is it?"

His question was like a pistol shot in the stillness.

Pastel shrieked, jumped, and spun to face him. "You—you scared me."

"You scared the hell out of me."

She stared at him. "How?"

"By not being here. By leaving a note with that crazy housekeeper—"

"You met Wilhelmina de Roos."

"Yes. She's nuts."

"She's a friend of Big Mike's and—"

"Oh, yeah? Let's see about that." He punched Mike's number into the hall phone, drumming his other hand on the wall while he waited.

"I left a note with your secretary," she muttered.

"I didn't find it until now. You should've insisted on being put through. . . . Yeah, Mike, Will. Tell me about Wilhelmina de Roos."

Pastel watched him, some of her tension draining away because he was there. Should she tell him?

"Yeah? Well, why didn't you tell me? She's the

mother from hell if you ask me. It's not funny, Mike. She knows what? Tae kwon do. Damn! She tries to throw me around this house, I'm not going to like it."

Despite her harrowing experience, Pastel felt her lips curl in a smile. He was a dynamo most of the time. Worried, he became a cyclone. What was it that had thrown him into a spin? He couldn't have known about the incident at the club. Or could he? Will Nordstrom was full of surprises.

He hung up the phone, facing her. "She checks out."

Pastel nodded.

"Why did you go to the club without me?"

"You were working."

"You could have waited."

She sighed. "You can't be in my pocket all the time, Will. You'll have to trust to your staff. We both have business lives—"

"I know that. I still need to know where you are."

"I'm not hiding from you."

"You're doing that when you go out and I don't know where you are."

Pastel decided not to tell him as she noted his agitation, the nervous way he ran his fingers through his hair, the tiny pearls of sweat on his upper lip. She loved him. There'd not be anyone like him again in this or any lifetime. She wouldn't kid herself about that anymore. Loving him meant protecting him as he was protecting her. He put himself on the line for her and the girls. She could do no less.

He hauled her into his arms. "Tell me next time."

"All right." There wouldn't be a next time.

"By the way," he said into her hair, "you were scared when you entered the house. Why?"

Mind scrambling, blood pulsing, she teetered on the edge of telling all. "Ah . . . the taxi driver said we'd been followed." When his grip tightened, her resolve hardened. Will was being driven crazy with her troubles. Sure, he was strong, tough. She knew that, reveled in it. But she was damned if she'd put him over the edge. "No, no. It wasn't bad. He explained that his ex-wife played games with him. The car turned off." She inhaled. "I just thought it would be a good idea to take precautions."

"You were white as a ghost."

"Didn't put on makeup," she lied. "And sometimes I'm that way after I exercise."

He pulled back, frowning down at her. "You're sure you're fine?"

"Yes."

Although he still looked doubtful, he left it at that, much to her relief.

That evening they stayed home and played a hotly contested game of Scrabble after dinner.

"That's not a word. You made that up, Will."

"Didn't. It's within the rights of man to coin words. I just did."

"You certainly did. Disjinmirred has a metallic ring to it. What does it mean? Did I pronounce it right?"

"No, you didn't, but since it's a word that will be used by undercover people, a code word, that's all right."

Pastel leaned back, arms crossed. "You think fast. I'll give you that."

"I hope you're not trying to impugn my integrity."

"Absolutely not. You don't have any when you play."

His eyes narrowed. "Have you been talking to my sisters?"

"Ah-ha! They think you're a cheat too."

"How could they? They're just poor losers, like you, who try to put a fellow like me down."

"Oh, you." She jumped up and raced around the table, leaning over him, pummeling him on the chest.

"Assault! I can have you arrested." Will twined his arms around her and pulled her down to his lap. "I demand recompense."

"I'll just bet you do." Cuddling close to him, she lifted her mouth, planting it on his. She felt his jerk of surprise. Then he took over, his mouth slanting over hers, his tongue tasting hers. He lifted his head, his eyes glassy.

"You sure there's nothing wrong," he said.

"What could be wrong?" She kissed him again.

"I don't know. My spine's quivering. Did that just before I met a kodiak."

"Did you run?"

"You don't run from bears. You curl up in a ball and hope they ignore you."

"You must've gotten away. You're here."

"It's not funny. You ought to see those guys. Bigger than barns, meaner than a drunken Klondike gold panner."

"You're exaggerating."

"And you're putting me off. What were we talking about?"

"This." Pastel kissed him again, her mouth open and seeking.

Will groaned, folding her into him.

In seconds they were hot, eager, wanting.

Holding her in his arms, Will carried her from the room, striding up the stairway that hugged one wall of the entryway. He hurried into the bedroom, not noticing the end of the coverlet that trailed on the floor. He put one foot on it, the other sliding under it. As he started to fall, he turned his body to protect Pastel and tumbled onto the bed with her on top of him.

"Have you been doing this romantic stuff very long?" she asked, giggling.

"Stop laughing. I am a romantic, I'll have you know."

"Graceful too."

He groaned.

Pastel cuddled him, feeling cherished and warm. Leaving him would be removing her heart right from the chest cavity.

"What is it?" he asked. "You groaned."

"Just excited." She couldn't hold back. She had to have him. She'd need the memories. Aggressive, wanting, she pulled at his clothes.

"Woman, you arouse the hell out of me."

"Me, too . . . I mean, you do—"

"Gotcha."

They couldn't get their clothes off fast enough.

"Pastel . . ."

"Will. I want to make love to you."

"Please do."

His hoarse voice delighted her as much as the hot look in his eyes did. She kissed him long and hard, determined to store up memories and shore up her decision to save him. He wanted to save her. Now it was her turn. Nothing was going to hurt him. Being away from him would be hell, but knowing he was safe would be the salve for that wound. Her resolve was cemented by the love she felt for him. For now, this minute, he was hers, and she was his. She was going to make it a night to remember with the man she knew she'd never forget. "Will, I love you."

"God! I can't get enough of hearing that."

"Good." Her mouth moved over his face, tasting, touching, committing it all to a sweet corner of her heart. Sliding her lips down his neck, she felt the rapid pulse beat in his throat, and exulted that she was the one to bring such heat to him.

"Pastel . . . Lord . . . honey, I'm in pieces."

"So am I. I'm not going to stop."

"Don't! I couldn't handle it."

Tenderness overwhelmed her, and she felt a tear slip down her face, drop on his chest.

"Darling?"

"I'm fine."

"You're crying."

" 'Cause I'm happy."

"So am I."

"I love you," she said again. She'd seen the hesitation, the questions. She couldn't let him ask. Her tongue roved his mouth, circling it, teasing, caressing, loving. . . .

Groaning, he kissed her, pressing his mouth hard to hers, parting her lips.

The violent passion shook her as her own rose to meet it. Never in her life had she expected such fire, nor did she figure it could be plumbed from her. She arched toward him, eliciting a groan from him.

"Love me, Pastel."

"I am."

In a sudden movement he turned her so that he could caress her breasts, taking the nipple into his mouth, worrying it with his tongue, letting it get pebble-hard.

"Don't . . . stop . . ." Her voice had a wail to it, as though he were her very salvation, her lifeline.

"I won't. There's much more loving between us."

"I want there to be."

A bizarre power filled her, as though she controlled destiny, that she was in charge of the universe. As though a light flashed on in her life, she knew she'd never be as afraid as she'd been before she met Will. He called her magic, but he was the sorcerer. Strength had been pumped into her. Her life would be a void without him, but she would be able to carry on.

"Come back to me."

"I'm here, Will. Always I'll be in your heart."

Lost in the silent, chaotic world of passion and desire, she gave herself to the wonderful spiral that whirled her away from the loneliness that would come soon enough. Knowing that the emptiness of her life would be magnified without Will, she pressed closer, wanting to be cemented to him. That she'd leave behind a piece of herself she knew. She wanted him to have it, just as she would take a portion of him. That was the only way she could survive.

Yet, as he loved her, she could feel herself melting, wanting to give in, stay with him. Only the girls, their protection, her need to keep Will from the nebulous threat that hung over her own life, firmed her resolve to leave.

Her body trembled, she whispered love words, her hunger growing. They strove to give each other maximum pleasure. In doing so, they brought themselves to the ultimate volcanic moment.

He entered her in slow moves.

She clutched him to her, wanting more.

Groaning in concert, moaning their joy, they came to orgasm in the smooth flight of angels, in a catastrophic joining.

"Pastel! I love you."

"And I love you."

Minutes passed. They fell asleep, still joined.

They woke and loved again.

The next morning Will was dressed and ready to go while Pastel had just finished showering. He had a breakfast meeting; she'd promised she'd take a cab to work.

He came into the bathroom, looking sophisticated, dangerous, and potent as hell. "I'll see you tonight. One last kiss." He felt her tremor. "What is it?" He stared into her eyes.

"Nothing. Just thinking about tonight." And she was. Being alone, wanting him, trying to escape him.

❖━━━━━━━━━❖

Not an hour later Pastel was on the road. She'd left a note for Will . . . her message obscure but the point about leaving him clear. She loved him too much to risk what could happen. He could be killed. The girl could be taken. She ended the letter with love and kisses.

As she was going out the door, her whole being told her to retreat. Then she recalled the arm around her neck, the choking steam. The girls! What would be done to them? It was as though their screams echoed in her head.

Getting her car from the garage at the back of the brownstone was almost a glitch. It wouldn't turn over. Since she usually used cabs while in New York, sometimes the battery got tetchy. Saying a prayer, she let it sit and tried again. Ignition!

She pulled into Manhattan traffic, then cursed the slow-moving bumper-to-bumper forward motion.

Finally she was out of the city proper.

Her foot jammed down on the accelerator, she entered the Holland Tunnel. At the turnpike entrance she snapped a ticket from the machine, honked her way past a slow mover, and floored it. Nothing was going to get in the way of escaping. She'd drive to Carlyle, get the girls, and head west. She had money in her checkbook. Her credit cards were clear. She could go a long way. And she knew how to hide.

Momentary regret for her modeling agency that would be sure to go belly-up had her hands tightening on the wheel. Maybe Will would take it over, make it a part of Brockman-Nordstrom.

"Fool!" she castigated herself. "He'll work on forgetting you."

Jamming at the buttons on her radio, she got Guns n' Roses blasting their way into her brain. She welcomed the ear-splitting cacophony.

The world skimmed past her as the road climbed into the foothills of the Catskills. Little by little the traffic thinned as she put some distance between her and the Big Apple.

Keeping her speed at ten miles above the limit, she prayed that the heavy patrol on New York's highways had been hit by budget cuts.

She proceeded through the mountains to a high plateau and Carlyle. The rarefied air of the mountains had been good for the girls. They were in all the sports, excelled at classes, and enjoyed themselves.

"We miss you, Mom," Althea had said on the last call.

"Yeah," Yasmin had concurred. "It would be more fun to do things with you. Can't wait for summer."

Summer! Where would they be then?

Willie Nelson sang an oldie about love, and never saying good-bye.

Pastel bit her lip to keep from crying.

She punched the buttons on her radio, switching stations until she found anything but country music. She didn't need more pathos.

Was Will still at his breakfast meeting? She sneaked a glance at her watch just as the siren started up behind her. In her rearview mirror she saw the state trooper's car closing fast, strobe flashing. "Oh, no."

TEN

Will couldn't concentrate. The negotiations to acquire another television station should have excited him. Instead, he felt itchy, unsure. He rose to his feet, ignoring the stares. "Excuse me. Carry on without me. Anchor, you know the drill."

"Sure." Anchor nodded, as nonplussed as the others.

Will strode through to his adjoining office and picked up the phone. Pastel wasn't at her office, so he called the house. Wilhelmina answered.

"Nope," she said. "Miz Marx hasn't been here for quite a while."

"Did she say she was going to a client's?"

"Nope."

"Did she mention her destination?"

"Nope."

"Did she mention anything?"

"Nope."

"All right. Thanks. I'll—"

"Left you a note though. Found it on your desk. Got your name on it."

"What? Read it."

"Don't know's I should. Right to privacy—"

"I'm giving my permission," Will said through his teeth.

"Okay . . . but, I'm pertiklar about certain—"

"Read it."

"Okay."

Will nearly bit through his tongue waiting.

"Here we are . . . 'Dear Will—' That's you—"

"Go on."

"Okay. Ah, let's see. 'I left because it's safer this way. I'll contact you sometime in the future. You are a wonderful person. You just don't understand how strong these people are, or what they might do. Love, Pastel.' That's it."

"Damn!"

"Well, I can't help it . . . wait. Another call's coming in. Your ring."

"Answer it, and put it on conference call—"

"Don't know how to do that."

"Take the damn call and have them call me at this number." Will gave it to her and slammed down the receiver. Putting his head in his hands, he whispered her name. Never had he felt so helpless. Where would he look? He had to find her.

Seconds later his phone rang.

He snatched it up. "Nordstrom."

"Will? It's Lars. I'm at the house. We got a call from one of Mike's people. They took a police call on their radio. Recognized the license number. Pastel's."

Will leaped to his feet. "Where?"

"Heading toward Carlyle. Mike's sending Dov along in case there's trouble."

"I hear you. I'm on my way. Let them know."

"Will?"

"Yeah?"

"She must be pretty frightened."

"Yeah." She was scared—and she didn't trust him. Hurt was a vinegar of the soul. "I'll talk to you later." He slammed down the phone and grabbed his briefcase and keys.

Anchor came through the connecting door, took one look at Will, then closed the door at his back. "It's going well in there. I'm letting them talk among themselves for a while. They'll convince themselves our offer is fabulous." The smile left his face. "How can I help?"

"Hold the fort. Keep in touch with Lars. Don't drop the ball in there."

"Right. Pastel?"

"She took off."

"Find her, Will. She's too good to lose."

"I know." He crossed the room to a closet. In

case of important business engagements, he stocked clothes. It hadn't happened often, but a few times, because of spills or the like, he'd needed to change. Not many of the clothes were sportswear, but there was one pair of jeans, some Reeboks, and a cotton shirt. He grabbed them.

He threw off his suit, tie, and dress shirt, tossing them on the couch. Dressing took mere minutes.

Anchor was hanging up his suit as Will slammed out of the office, running to the elevator. "Good luck," he whispered.

Will had no patience with the traffic and took a few chances, getting out of Manhattan as fast as he could. Prudent enough not to call down the scrutiny of the troopers, as Pastel must have done, he scooted in and out of cars, making progress, though he cursed every lost second. Horns blared around him as drivers took exception to his Chinese-tag progress on the city's congested roads.

Once he was on the highway, he had relatively clear sailing. Using his car phone, he called Mike and told him his plans. Mike said he would handle everything, and added that Dov was about fifteen minutes away from Carlyle. Will said he'd keep in touch and hung up.

Pastel must have been very agitated to speed, he thought as he zipped past a semi. She didn't want confrontations with the police. He could recall how careful she'd been to avoid such things, how upset she'd been when he'd called Mike to watch her, to try to find who was menacing her. They hadn't found the bastards yet. He would. He was damn well going to wipe the fear from her life. She'd been more or less hiding for years, avoiding any contact with those who might upset her plan . . . safety for the girls at any price. Now she was putting her life on the line again . . . to save his.

Will ground his teeth. She'd been under a black-mailer's thumb for years, but she never called it that. Hell! She probably didn't consider the bond-age of her life in that light. But it was. Whoever was keeping her hanging, twisting in the wind like some trophy, was going to pay, big-time.

Why hadn't she trusted him? Scanning a map propped on the dash, he headed for Route 17, his foot to the floor.

Pastel saw the school. It sat high on the side of a foothill, The Carlyle School for Young Ladies, the largest employer in the tiny hamlet.

She drove down into the town, to the one stop-light on the main street, and decided to get a bagel at the local diner before facing Dr. Myabelle Lewiston, headmistress of Carlyle. Born in Oxford, Missis-sippi, and convinced there were any number of women who could outwrite Faulkner, she'd come to the Catskill Mountains to prove her point. Pastel had been impressed on first meeting. She'd given the girls into her care with little trepidation. Dr. Lewiston was a redoubtable believer in right, and she'd move one of the Catskills to protect her students.

Pastel parked, getting out and stretching her muscles. She sniffed the fresh, crisp air and thought of Lake Placid. No! Don't think of Will.

The diner wasn't too cool, but it was a far way from hot. Some of the patrons had their heavy jackets on as they ate. Three ceiling fans kept the air moving, spreading what heat there was along the narrow room.

Pastel gazed around, sniffing. Succulent aromas stirred her dormant appetite. The baked goods, looking fresh and flaky, sat behind glass. The smell of bacon, sausage, eggs, and toast were pleasant, but didn't appeal to her nervous innards.

She ordered a bagel, cream cheese, and a glass of skim milk. She chewed each bite twenty times, sipped her milk, struggling to keep her chaotic thoughts at bay. She couldn't dwell on the future. It hurt. The immediate past held fear and wrenching loss. Concentrating on the moment, what she had to do in the next hour, kept her head straight.

She'd almost finished her repast when she felt the gaze. Not turning, she wiped her hands on the napkin, and let it settle in her lap. On the pretext of ordering coffee, she looked up into the mirror over the serving bar. No one . . . except a very old man and a younger one with a tool belt hanging low on his middle. The door clanged shut. Her gaze flew to it. She could make out the form of a man through the frosted glass. She caught only the sheen of blue-black hair. Had he been watching her?

Shaken, she wiped her now-damp hands, signaled for her bill, and rose. After paying, she hugged her capacious bag in front of her and left the diner. The ringing of the bell over the door jarred her.

Looking both ways, she headed for her car, parked at the curb. Head down, she got in, locked the door, then gazed around her. She must have imagined it. No one was in her vicinity. She'd caught no unfriendly gaze.

He spotted her by accident. Barreling into the hamlet after coming off several miles of a winding, hilly two-lane road, he braked hard when he saw the stoplight at the four corners just ahead. Damn. Any holdup had him spitting tacks.

He glanced around, saw the coffee shop. Should he make time for takeout? No. Better get to the school.

Then she was there! In front of him, coming out of the diner, looking around.

He stiffened. Had someone approached her? She looked harried as she fumbled for her keys. She scrutinized the street again, but didn't spot his car, idling as it was behind a cement mixing truck. Dammit! She looked worried.

His own gaze swept the area. Had she seen something? Someone?

Intent as he was, he almost missed it when she pulled away. The horn sounding behind him signaled the green light. She was gone! No. She'd turned left, going up the hill. Then he saw what he was sure was the school. A campus and buildings that would have done credit to a small college. First rate. It had to cost a bundle.

Gritting his teeth, he followed her, not exploding into speed as he was tempted. He wasn't going to lose her now. He needed to know her plan, what she intended to do, before he acted. Damn Pastel Marx for scaring him. And curse her predators. He'd deal with them. He'd drag them across the Alaskan tundra and leave them to freeze.

As he made his way up the winding drive, he noticed the sun slanted in longer shadows across the snow-covered ground. Here and there were students building snowmen, or riding down the slopes on pieces of cardboard. Carefree, unafraid, the way students should be.

He ground his teeth at what Pastel had gone

through to give some measure of safety and normalcy to Althea and Yasmin.

Snow was piled high on both sides of the drive, but the sky was clear, vivid blue, everything having a diamond clarity. Up ahead, at the top of the curve in the drive, was a brick building that must be Administration. Other brick buildings dotted the area around it. Off to the left was a tennis court banked in snow. Beyond was a structure that looked like it housed a pool. Alongside the administration building was another with double doors. The sign just clearing the snowbank said DAPHNE DALRYMPLE LIBRARY.

Will parked alongside the road, choosing to walk up the rest of the incline. Pastel's car was there, in the small parking lot in front of the administration building.

He went up the wide steps two at a time, inhaling a deep breath of frosty air before pushing open the glass door. There was a rush of welcoming warmth. Spring was on the way, but winter was being stubborn.

Pausing just inside the door, he studied the two-story entry. A wide stairway up the middle, corridors on either side. Several doors opening from the lobby. His glance skated off, then caught the sign ADMINISTRATION over the first door to the left. The upper part of the door was clear glass. He looked through. There was Pastel. She was speaking to a woman who was holding open a door to an inner office. She was almost as tall as Pastel. Iron-gray hair cut short and close to the head, a purposeful chin, a no-nonsense wool suit, convinced Will she was the person in charge.

Pastel went past her; the women closed the door behind them.

Will waited a few seconds, then pushed open the door to the outer office.

A woman looked up and smiled. "May I help you?"

"Is this the headmistress's office?"

"Yes." She glanced at the closed door. "I'm afraid she's busy at the moment. Did you have an appointment?"

"No."

She inclined her head, her smile regretful. "I'm sorry . . ."

"No need to be." Will crossed the room to the inner office.

"Sir! Sir, don't. You can't go in there."

"I can."

He shoved open the door and smiled at the two women who looked askance at him.

"Will!" Pastel exclaimed.

"That's right. What are you doing here?"

"I have an . . . what are *you* doing here?"

"Stopping you from making a mistake. I've spent a hell of a morning and a damned tough ride to get here. Explain yourself."

Stung, Pastel glared. "Stuff yourself." She caught the interested glance of the headmistress. "Forgive me. I thought we'd be—"

"Don't worry," Dr. Lewiston said. She addressed Will.

"How do you do? I'm Myabelle Lewiston. I take it you're here because you've interested yourself in the lives of Althea and Yasmin Donnelly." He nodded. "You may sit down, unless Mrs. Donnelly objects."

Her inquiring look snapped Pastel out of her shock. "Ah . . . yes . . . I mind . . ."

"Pastel!" Will said. "I mean it. Don't screw around. This is serious."

"You think I don't know that." White-faced, she stared at him. "I'm leaving. So are the girls."

"Not without me."

Tight-lipped, Dr. Lewiston fixed on Pastel. "Unless they are going to a school with a good reference for learning, I wouldn't approve moving them."

Will shot her a hard look. "They're going to Alaska. They'll be taught in my sister's school not far from Anchorage. It's a fine school with first-class instructors. My sister has a master's from Juilliard. Most of the staff have master's or doctorates."

"Alaska?" Pastel half rose out of her chair. "You can't just—"

"I have. Whatever the hell is bugging you will

have to go on hold. I think you'll agree the girls come first."

"I do . . . but—"

"No buts. They'll be in Alaska tomorrow. My mother, brother, and sisters will accompany them, plus an assortment of bodyguards. Their itinerary will be secret, except to us. They'll be out of the way. Then I'll settle with the rest of it."

"Just like that?"

"You got it."

"Do you know what you're dealing with? No, you don't." Pastel shook her finger in his face. "You can't believe the power they have."

"And you haven't seen mine."

"Excuse me," Dr. Lewiston said. "Will one of you please explain what is happening here."

Pastel pressed her lips together. "It's a long story."

"Synopsize it, then."

In brief, brittle sentences, Pastel told the headmistress about her life with the girls. "Now," she finished, "I think they're in immediate danger. That's why I have to run."

"The government could help," Dr. Lewiston said.

"Did they stop the bombing of the Trade Center?" Pastel spread her hands. "People enter this country every day, then disappear, to surface again as terrorists. Do you think our government would take the time, or man the personnel, to monitor two girls who may or may not be in danger?"

"But you think they are."

"I know they are. I couldn't prove it to the authorities. In the meantime, Althea and Yasmin could be kidnapped and never heard of again."

Dr. Lewiston nodded. "How can I help?"

Pastel stared at the other woman, tears beginning to trail down her cheeks, her throat working as she fought to stop the flow.

"It's been rough," Will said, his gaze sliding away from Pastel to the headmistress.

"I've survived rough times before."

Will smiled briefly. "I have to believe whoever wants the girls knows they're here. Now that Pastel has run, they'll come looking."

Dr. Lewiston sank back in her chair, smiling. "Let them. Carlyle may look like a sleepy village with outdated attitudes, but the people hereabouts are devoted to me and this school. I've educated their children, and tutored the ones with problems, no charge. I have an army, Mr. . . .what is your name?" Even as she asked, she lifted the phone. "Dina, get me Jonas Sloan. Now. Wherever he is."

"Nordstrom. Will."

"All right, Nordstrom, Will, you and Mrs. Donnelly get Althea and Yasmin. I'll have one of the dorm monitors help them pack. My army will take it from there. I assure you they'll take instant umbrage at the thought of outsiders trying to . . . bother us." She stood up. "I suggest you get moving."

Pastel nodded. "Thank you. We will."

She and Will left the office, watching each other warily.

"You'll have to tell me what set you off," Will said after a moment.

"I don't."

"I was damned afraid."

She looked down at her feet. "I'm sorry. It couldn't be helped—"

"So you've said. I disagree."

She looked away from him.

Silence reigned until one of the dorm monitors clattered down the stairs and gestured for them to follow her.

"No one, not parent, relative, sibling, or friend can just rattle through the halls of Carlyle without an escort," she said proudly. "I'm Jane, and I'll be with you until you leave the school. Dr. Lewiston is very firm about taking precautions."

"I approve," Will told her.

Jane beamed, chattering on about the school, its age, its high level of academe.

"Now what?"

Pastel's question, out of the blue, had him turning toward her. "Pastel, you're angry, but so am—"

"I'm not angry. I'm apprehensive. You're so sure of yourself. What makes you think they haven't the jump on us?"

"Look—"

"In the diner I was sure I was being watched."

Will cursed. Jane turned, frowning.

"Is there a phone?" he asked.

"Right next to Yasmin and Althea's room, just down the hall here."

"Thanks, Jane," Pastel said. "I'll go with you. Mr. Nordstrom will catch up."

Will strode quickly to the phone. Pastel and Jane continued on the few feet to the girls' room as he dialed Mike's number.

"Mike," he said when the other man answered. "I'm at Carlyle. Can you get in touch with Dov? Pastel thought someone was watching her at the diner here in town. Tell him to look around."

Pastel tried to listen to Will's conversation, but Althea and Yasmin suddenly bounced out of their room.

"Mom! Hi!"

"Hi yourself." She opened her arms, and the two dark-haired girls catapulted into them, throwing her out of balance. The joy of holding them, knowing they were safe, brought tears to her eyes. Her grip tightened. She fought for control. "Thanks, Jane."

"How come you're here?" Yasmin asked, squirming free.

Pastel sighed, looking at them both. "I'm afraid you have to leave Carlyle. For a little while," she added quickly when they groaned. "Jane and I will help you pack."

"Come on, girls," Jane said, heading into the room.

The girls followed her reluctantly. Pastel straightened and started after them, but Will's hand on her arm stopped her. She looked up at him, and he pulled her into his embrace.

"You scared the hell out of me," he said.

"Nice talk," she mumbled into his chest. She gripped his shirt with both hands. "I thought I was doing the right thing."

He kissed her hard. "You weren't. Now we'll do it." He kissed her again, then lifted his head. "Together. We can handle it."

She nodded. "Actually, I'd prefer it. I didn't know what we were going to do when we left, or where we were going. Just run. That was the plan."

"Not a good one."

"I guess not." She palmed her hand over his cheek. "Your move, Batman."

"All right, Robin. You go downstairs. I'm going to introduce myself to the girls."

"Oh. Maybe I should—"

"No need. We've talked on the phone. We just haven't met face-to-face."

Pastel didn't know whether to laugh or protest when he turned her around and pointed.

"You wait down there. We'll be along."

"Right." It was far easier to acquiesce.

In minutes she heard the clamor, laughing, talking, and a thumping that sounded like suitcases against the wall. Yasmin and Althea leaped down the stairs, chattering at the same high, laughing pitch.

"We're going to be Alaskans," Althea announced.

Pastel's smile faltered. "Are you?"

"Yes," Yasmin answered. "And we're going in a helicopter. Then a plane. Wish you were coming."

"Helicopter? Alone?" Pastel grasped at the one word she'd heard in all the jumble. She looked up at Will trundling two steamer trunks, a custodian behind him with smaller luggage.

"Need help, Will?"

"Thanks for asking, Althea. You're a little late."

She and Yasmin laughed.

"Tell me more about this trip," Pastel said.

"We leave today. We'll take classes up north." Althea looked important.

Will was moving mountains again. "I think we need to discuss—"

"Oh, here's Linda, our proctor, Mom."

The door to Administration snapped open. Dr. Lewiston smiled at Pastel, then eyed the proctor and Will. "Miss Martin, would you come in here, please. Mr. Nordstrom, you as well."

"I'll come too," Pastel said.

"No need, Mrs. Donnelly. I know the girls are eager to visit with you."

"But I—"

"I'll handle it," Will told her, kissing her on the cheek.

"I'm their mother," she said through her teeth.

"Sure, you are," Will soothed. Then he followed Linda Martin and Dr. Lewiston."

"Don't worry, Mom, Will can handle anything."

"*Et tu*, Althea?" Pastel muttered.

Yasmin squinted at her. "Are you in a snit, Mom?"

"No." Pastel's grin twisted. "I can't win against an Alaskan."

"Yeah. And we're going there! Can you beat it?"

"No, I don't think I can," Pastel muttered, glancing over her shoulder at the door marked ADMINISTRATION.

ELEVEN

"Why didn't you tell me what Dr. Lewiston said right away?"

"It wasn't that important, Pastel. And I've just told you. Linda Martin, as proctor, was told that all arrivals on campus would be scrutinized more carefully than usual. And that, yes, some outsiders were noticed in town. That was the message for me."

"I should've been in on that."

"There wouldn't have been any need if you'd stayed here, where you belong."

"You are damn well blowing out the windows with your bellowing." Pastel paced the living room of Will's town house. "I won't be yelled at like some . . . some—"

"I wasn't yelling," Will roared. "I was telling you something."

"You were howling like a damned banshee."

Neither heard the door open behind them, but both turned at the sound of Helborg's voice.

"What's going on, Will? You're bawling like a wounded bull elk." Helborg's bland assessment turned his fulminating son beet red, and elicited a reluctant laugh from Pastel. "I always knew it would be like this for you too."

"Father, I'd like to speak to Pastel alone."

"Really? I thought you were showing her how to call hogs."

Pastel laughed again, unbending a bit.

Helborg smiled at her.

Will glowered. "We were settling something."

"What? The Civil War?"

Pastel didn't try to contain her mirth.

Helborg looked pleased, beaming at her. "I like a girl with a sense of humor."

"I like a man with one," she retorted, smiling wider when he guffawed.

"I feel I'm in the way here—" Will began at his most caustic.

Helborg nodded. "Astute of you to notice. Must be good for you living in Manhattan, Will. You used to be dull and not too perceptive."

"Now, that's funny," Pastel murmured, her chin lifting when Will's brows met over his nose, and he glowered at her.

"Thank you. I live to amuse." Will turned on

his heel and strode from the room, slamming the door behind him.

Helborg gestured to Pastel to take a seat next to the fireplace.

"I think your son's angry with you," she said. She was still angry with Will. What shook her, though, was how she enjoyed going toe to toe with him. A lifetime of avoiding confrontations had not prepared her for the sweet cleansing of a verbal blowout. Fighting had never appealed to her, and letting insults fly was a tacky exercise in futility. But, airing differences, defending a point of view, was refreshing, exhilarating.

"And more angry with you," Helborg said.

She nodded, not meeting his eyes.

"He'll get over it. I wanted to tell you something. I couldn't wait."

"Oh?"

"Will's mad about you."

Pastel was speechless for a minute. Whatever she'd expected him to say, it certainly wasn't that. "Mr. Nordstrom—"

"Helborg."

"Yes . . . well . . . Helborg." She took a deep breath, but couldn't think of anything else to say.

"You love him, I think," Helborg went on. "And Will loves the girls too."

Pastel fell back in her chair. "Just like that."

He nodded. "I'm sorry I didn't get to meet Althea and Yasmin, but nothing will get to them, or get through my family. That's my vow to you."

In the grip of the terrible weakness of fearful parenthood, Pastel could only shake her head. One tear coursed down her cheek. "I know you'd keep them safe, that Will is stalwart . . . and that I love him." She sighed, wiping her cheeks. "Who keeps him safe?"

"He's tough, as canny as hell, and unafraid—"

"I know. He's Alaskan."

"Right."

"He's not bulletproof." She bit her lip on a sob.

Helborg leaned forward, patting her knee. "No, he isn't." He exhaled, his cheeks bellowing out. "I suppose I shouldn't tell you . . . I'm going to." He lowered his voice. "Will and Mike think they have a line on the people who've been harrowing you."

Pastel made a sound in her throat. "I think I've known from the beginning who it was." She couldn't look in his face. "You must think me pretty rotten that I haven't shared this with Will."

"I think you're a mother desperate to protect your children."

She looked back at him. "I've—I've made a mess of it."

Helborg shook his head. "Maybe you should've trusted Will more. I can understand the fear that drove you." He leaned forward. "Who is it?"

"I'm sure it's my friend's husband, Ibn. I'm positive he's the one who offered his daughters to the sheikh in the first place, to use to gain some mineral rights."

"Your friend's husband was so unconscionable as to do this?"

Pastel hesitated. She'd never had much use for Ibn, thinking him lazy, manipulative. But would he truly have done that? "I never thought of him as being without principle, just a man who always took the easy road."

"Maybe he isn't the one."

Pastel shook her head. "He must be. He's the only one—"

"Who could've condemned his wife and daughters to death?"

The harsh declarative that she'd never even voiced in her mind shook her. "Yes," she muttered.

Helborg patted her knee as the door opened. "Wait until we catch them. Then you'll know for sure."

"Am I interrupting?" Will asked sarcastically.

Helborg laughed. "You're in quite a state, my son."

Will reddened. "I had a call from Mike. He says they might've boxed them in. He called a friend at the State Department and talked to him."

Pastel shook her head. "What are you talking about?"

Will moved his shoulders, his gaze skating off her. "The immunity thing. If there's some question over the disappearance of Pam . . . her death . . . I'm sorry . . ."

Pastel nodded. "I know. Go on."

"If there's a question, there might be something that can fall into the realm of international negotiation. Mike said that his friend mentioned the policy of withholding funds from certain areas when it's a case of terrorism. Whether this fits the bill is another story. It's done as leverage. Nahumi could come up short on a trade deal with us if it's proved that an American who'd gone to the country to perform humanitarian services was set upon, kidnapped, or otherwise harassed." Will glanced at Pastel. "It might not work out. It's just a chance." He spun around and left the room.

Helborg looked at her. "He's hurting."

"So am I," she blurted out, then reddened when he laughed.

"You might have to soothe some ruffled feathers."

"I can do that," she murmured.

The long pause between them wasn't uncomfortable. Pastel liked Will's forthright family, who seemed to think that open affection was normal.

"Why?"

Startled, she looked up at Will's father. "Why what?"

"Why did you run? You had a scare in Lake Placid and didn't bolt. You come home, and bang. Something kicked it off, and it had to've been frightening."

Pastel gnawed at her bottom lip. She shouldn't talk about it. Then she blurted it out. "I went to the athletic club to work out . . ." The story poured out of her.

"Lord! The bastard. You have no idea who it was?"

"None. I didn't recognize the voice. That's not unusual. Often I've had calls and the voices were strange."

"You're saying it's quite a network."

"That would be my guess."

Later that evening, when Pastel was readying for bed in the master bedroom of Will's town house, she heard Will in the bathroom. Like a flashback she recalled that first day in the chalet, when she'd walked in on him after his shower. She trembled, not with fear, but with desire. The need to love him, to clear away their misunderstandings, to be one with each other, was so potent, she reeled with it.

Torn by amusement, trepidation, and desire, she eyed the closed door as she heard the sound of the shower.

Helborg was right, she loved Will. And he loved her. She could keep him.

After stripping off her clothes, she strode to the door, hoping he hadn't locked it.

The knob turned. Out of breath, off balance, but confident she was doing the right thing, she pushed open the door.

Will wasn't whistling. He was humming. "Amazing Grace!" Good Lord! He was in a mood. Wasn't that played at funerals? Or maybe it was weddings.

She could see through the frosted glass door. Though it was opaque, the overhead light outlined him. Head up, he was facing the water, letting it sluice over that beautiful body. Oh, how she wanted it.

For the first time in many years she could look into the future, and hope, yearn, plan. She'd fight to get it, and battle to keep it.

Taking a deep breath, she slid back the door, knowing the instant he felt the cool blast, and was turning. "Hi. Thought I'd shower with you."

His face covered in soap, he tried to see, one eye squinted. "Pastel?"

"You were expecting Madonna?"

"No . . . no."

"Well, then."

He reached out a hand. "Come in."

He rinsed the soap off as she stepped into the tub. When he turned to her, his gaze slid over her, lingering on her breasts, her hips. Heat built like a forest fire inside her.

"I—I thought I'd wash," she said.

"Me too." He never took his eyes off her.

"Maybe we should hurry."

"Good idea."

"Getting a cold?" She gulped a laugh.

"Getting aroused."

"Me too."

"Lord!"

"You're still hoarse."

"I'm lucky my voice is working at all. The rest of me is in shock."

"Not all." She grinned, gazing at definite signs of excitement.

A smile lurked at his mouth. "Looks like you're in a mood."

"I am."

"So am I."

After he finished washing and left, she leaned against the tile, trying to cool her face. "My, he's beautiful."

She hurried through her own washing, then cursed herself for shampooing too. She'd done it while mooning over Will. "Damn." Her heavy hair took too long to dry.

Wrapping her head in a towel, she used oil on her wet skin, then dried it. She shook her hair free and looked in the mirror. "Great. A witch, if you please."

Swiping at the lank strands, she put the dryer on full.

"Here, let me do that," Will said from the doorway.

Her eyes snapped open. "Takes so long," she said weakly. He enthralled her. He was naked and gorgeous.

"Yeah. I like doing it."

She stood with her back to him, feeling his hardness, wishing her foolish hair would dry so she could hold him, so she could love him, show him how much of her life was linked to his. "Have I told you how much I love making love with you? You showed me beauty in lovemaking. I'd thought there was nothing to sex except discomfort. Not true. It's a paradise that can't be explained. You let me live it. You brought me out of hiding. I could look at myself, at my situation, and have the guts to change certain aspects of my life that I thought were irrevocable. If I had nothing else to thank you for, there would be a great deal of gratitude just in that.

"I don't want your gratitude."

"Well, you're going to get it, Nordstrom, so don't interrupt."

"I'd rather go to bed."

"We'll do that. I need to tell you this."

"All right."

She turned as he put the dryer down, and she smiled at the heat in his eyes. He wanted her.

Good. She was hungry for him. "You've turned my life around. I don't know the exact moment, or how you did it. You just did. I lost a lot of the fear. . . . No, that's not right. I didn't lose it. It's still with me." She took a deep breath. "You let me channel it into positive energy. I'd been existing in very negative fashion, back-pedaling to keep the wolves away. Instead, they became bolder, more sure of their ability to keep me in line. Now I know I don't have to live according to their specifications."

"Not anymore."

She smiled. "You did that."

"Thanks." He reached for her. "You left me."

"Yes." She stared into his eyes, not pretending to misunderstand. He'd been badly hurt by what she'd done. He deserved an explanation. "I'd discovered a level of courage I didn't know I had. And—"

"What? It was wrong. It didn't take courage. It took stupidity."

She bristled. "Don't call me stupid."

"The act. Not the person."

"Nice pickup."

"Thanks. I used to play ball."

The smile hovering around his mouth disappeared and his expression grew stern. "Now lay it out for me. Why did you leave me? And how the hell could you think it a smart move?"

Chin up, she gave him her frostiest glare. "I decided I wanted to protect you as you've done for me. I knew it would hurt you, but I wanted to keep you safe, out of harm's way."

Will swept her into his arms, his mouth slamming onto hers with all the fierce gentleness that searching for her had roused in him. Eons later he moved his mouth to her ear, his blood thundering. "Then don't leave me. That can make me damned vulnerable. Hell, it could kill me."

She curled her arms around his neck, fitting herself to him. "I know how that feels."

"Don't do it again."

"I won't."

They stared at each other, so close their breaths commingled. He lifted her hand and kissed her fingers.

"I don't suppose," he murmured, "you're going to tell me what you talked to my father about."

She shook her head, barely able to concentrate as he sucked on her index finger. "He's very protective of you, you know. And I'm sure I'll be the same with our children."

Will gaped at her. "Children? You want..." He pulled her into his arms, hugging her tightly. "Oh, God. I was hoping you would." He leaned back from her, grinning. "I'd like more girls. Yours are beautiful."

"You'll take what you get. However many, whatever gender, we'll love them. They'll be happy."

"We'll all be happy." He leaned down and

scooped her up into his arms. "You still have time to tell me to bug off," he said as he carried her into the bedroom.

She curled her arms around his neck, blowing in his ear. When she saw his frown, she was confused. "What?"

"I didn't get much chance to meet the girls. They'll know their cousins, aunts, uncles, and grandmother better than they do me."

Hiccuping a laugh, she pressed her face into his neck. "Jumping the gun as usual."

He lowered her to the bed. "If you won't marry me, will you live with me?"

She looked up as him. "Who said I wouldn't marry you? You shouldn't have children without marriage—"

"You're pregnant!" he shouted, hugging her. He rolled over so she was on top on him and grinned like a fool, patting her back. "We'll take every precaution. You shouldn't—"

"Wait! Easy, Thunder. I'm not pregnant. I was just stating my preferences for motherhood."

"Oh."

His disappointment tore a chuckle from her. When he looked sulky, she put her head on his chest. "I'd love a child. But I'd like to take it in order."

"Then let's take it in order. Marry me."

She lifted her arm, put it across his chest, and

leaned her chin on it. "Maybe we should clean up the mess in my life first."

"That could take a few weeks. I don't want to wait."

"A few weeks?"

"No more. I mean it. . . . Hey! Don't cry."

"I'm not. I'm just a little weepy because I'm feeling secure."

Will's gaze narrowed. His hands turned questing. "You could be pregnant. My sister got downright foolish when she was that way and—"

"Nordstrom!"

"Yes?"

"I'm not . . . but I wouldn't mind."

"I love you."

"I know. I love you too."

"Will you marry me?"

"Before we settle all this?"

"Yes . . . or right after." He turned her over so he could look down into her eyes.

"All right."

He went very still. " 'All right' meaning what?"

"Let's get married . . . now."

He closed his eyes. "You won't change your mind?"

"Nope."

"I feel weak as a kitten."

"Too bad. I'm aroused."

He opened one eye. "I can handle it."

"I hope so. It's too late in the evening to get a surrogate."

"That's not funny."

"Was too. I have a great sense of humor."

"You're a sadist."

Pastel laughed out loud, happy, more passion-filled than she thought possible.

Will leaned over her, smiling. "You are such a nut when you're unafraid." He cocked his head.

"What?"

"I was wondering if it would be as sexy to make love to you now that you're tough as a bear."

"Tougher than a bear . . . and I'll be twice as sexy."

"You've got my interest."

She hauled his head down to her. "I want to make love to you."

"Feel free."

She grinned. "You're too big to turn over . . . and I should be on top."

Laughter burst from him. Accommodating her, he moved from her onto his back. "There."

"Thanks." Leaning on his chest, she studied him. "Is there anything you don't know about making love?"

"Huh?" Surprised, he blinked.

Pleased, she put her chin near his. "I want to be innovative. I don't have the track record you have—"

"Now, wait a minute. I'm no bed hopper, Pastel Marx-Donnelly, and I don't collect coup along the way."

"Really?" She looked down at her fingers playing on his chest, not wanting him to see the pleased gleam in her eye. "I'll bet you're a real Alaskan stud."

"Pastel . . . dammit . . . you're embarrassing me. I like women. Always have." He glared at her, then sighed. "All right. I'll admit that if I'd known there was someone like you in the world, that I'd meet you, that I would've had a chance of keeping you, I would've . . . lived in another way."

"Ah-ha, you were a skirt chaser!"

"I was not," he retorted, more stung than he thought he could be. "I was a normal—"

"Hah!"

"I was." In his mind's eye, all those flings and chases took on the aspect of a crazed teenager's bout with hormonal explosion. "I might've backed off quite a few if I'd known about you. We don't get to see into the future."

"You should've gambled that you'd meet me and been more circumspect."

"Circumspect? Good Lord . . . listen, I wasn't all that bad." He frowned. "Don't talk to my sisters."

Enjoying herself, miffed at those other women who'd had his attention, yet finding his dilemma delicious, she tried to look wounded. "I, on the other hand, was leading a most exemplary life—"

"First altar girl in America, no doubt," he muttered.

"Tsk-tsk. Mustn't be dyspeptic—"

"Dyspeptic? Where the hell did that archaic word spring from?"

"Me."

When she grinned like a little girl, his heart turned over, and he knew that he had to marry her that moment. "Let's get married tomorrow."

"I'd like nothing better." She reached to the side table and waved a note at him. "Anchor called and said he'd meet us tomorrow night at the Waldorf for the kickoff party . . . whatever that is. . . ."

Will clamped a hand to his forehead. "I forgot."

"Shame."

"If you have so much magic, why don't you make the Waldorf disappear?"

"Did you mutter what I think you did?"

"Maybe."

"Did you say I was magic? That I should make the Waldorf disappear? Wow, what've you been drinking?"

"Nothing. But I might have one."

Before he could turn away, she took his hand. "You called me magic. Did you mean it?"

"Oh, yeah. I meant it." He cupped her face in

his hands. "Everything about you is touched by the stars, Pastel. You're the only one who doesn't know it."

Shaken, she could only stare into his eyes. "You're crazy."

"I am about you. I'm not wrong about your potency, love. You have a way of turning things the right way. You almost lost yourself by sacrificing so much. Maybe because you're willing to chance it for others, your whole being has expanded. It shines out of you. I like being in the glow. I'd guess that's a big part of your magnetism. You're very loving, and I love you for it. Your looks alone belong in a fantasy. You're sexy, beautiful, and kind."

She gulped, overwhelmed by his description, humbled by his openness, awed at the depth of his feeling. "That describes you, Nordstrom."

"Thank you, ma'am." He kissed the end of her nose. His mouth slid down and fastened to hers. "Did I mention I was aroused too?"

"I guessed."

In moments, the levity, the talking, evaporated. Building passion pushed everything aside. They were alone in a world of sensation, caught in a web of emotion that pulled them, cherished them, gave them their own world.

Will trailed a series of kisses down her side, rubbing his lips over her breasts, taking a nipple into his mouth, circling it with his tongue, sucking there. His hands were questing, feathering over her skin, the feel of her making his libido climb, his blood cascade.

His hand touched her woman's place, and felt the moistness. She was ready for him. "Pastel."

"Yes."

"I can't say I love you enough."

"Neither can I."

The taste of her was intoxicating. She heated him to melting.

Lost in his touch, Pastel could only gasp when his mouth moved down her body. She wanted more . . . she wanted to give more.

When he moved to the soft triangle of her womanhood, she quivered, arched, as though her body had taken over from her mind. As though it were hinged to him, it writhed closer. A moan tore from her throat.

His tongue teased the nub at the opening. She bloomed like a flower. It was his turn to groan. "Pastel, you're so hot."

"Yes." Fuzzily she wondered why he was surprised. She'd told him she was.

His tongue entered the soft, slick opening, delving deep.

Whirling in the great, hot flurry of flooding passion, she clung to him, murmuring her desire for more . . . more. Everything in her tensed in anticipation for the coming wonder, for the voyage only lovers take, over the barrier that love alone can master, into the explosive heat of physical joining. More than a melding, beyond connection, it was a cementing of souls, a rush of blazing ecstasy that consumed, entangled, and freed.

Thrashing back and forth, she tried to tell Will . . . now! Now! She'd climbed so high. She whirled above the earth, needing the culmination yet wanting to extend the final moment. Frenzied, happy, she clung to him, and knew she'd never let him go.

Now, Will.

As though her soul's voice resonated over them, he moved up her body, sliding into her.

"Will!"

"I'm with you."

"I know. Don't leave me."

"Not a chance," he said, his voice hoarse, the words a commitment, a vow.

Driving toward fulfillment, they felt the first rush. Embracing, they took it, and gave back, went with it. Eager, seeking the other's joy, giving of self, they climbed the mountain. They found it all.

TWELVE

Pastel was excited. They were going out together. A date. She knew they were both adults, not teenagers, but she felt as though it were prom night. But not one of the dances she'd attended when she was younger had exhilarated her as much. She'd be with Will!

Giggling, her hand over her mouth, she smiled at herself in the bathroom mirror. It was crazy. She felt young . . . without a care . . . eager. She couldn't recall a time since college that she had.

The girls were safe. No one could get to them. Alaskans wouldn't let them. The certainty gave a lightness and anticipation to the evening she'd never experienced. Dreams could come true.

"I can let my hair down," she told the bathroom mirror.

Then she grimaced. Her hair. She was going to

have to do it herself. There were no assistants as she'd have at a shoot.

It took quite a time to do her hair the way she wanted. A braid, twisted to a coronet atop her head. A tendril of hair touched her ears on each side. Gold twists caught with rubies and coral were her earrings. The thin strands of hair seemed to weave with the earrings, catching the light. Outrageously expensive . . . and borrowed through the good offices of Anchor Bliss, the jewelry would have to be returned that evening to a safe.

She touched the lavaliere at her throat. It was a larger piece than she usually wore, but it was so intricate, so curved and airy-looking, it didn't seem to have any weight at all.

Finishing her makeup, she donned filmy underwear and stockings. Time for the dress. Flipping a silk wrapper around her shoulders, she left the roomy bathroom, stopping short in the bedroom. "Wilhelmina!"

The older woman grimaced at her. "I'll give you a hand, but I'm no shakes at this dressy stuff."

"Ah, thanks. That's all right. I'll manage."

Wilhelmina planted her feet apart and glared at the dress hanging to one side of the wide dressing table. "I'll help. Said I would."

Her stolid answer almost made Pastel chuckle.

"All right." She went past the woman, took the dress, and dropped the robe.

Wriggling into the coral sheath she'd worn the first time she'd met Will took time. It was tight and form-fitting from neck to hem. "Perhaps if you could just handle the zipper . . . ?"

Wilhelmina snapped it up, then stood back. "Glory be."

"How do I look?" Pastel turned in front of the mirror.

"Shameless."

Laughter broke from her. "Surely not that bad."

"Worse. My mother would've shot me if I wore such a rig. 'Course, I admit, it would've ripped when I yanked it over my thighs."

Laughing, Pastel shook her head. "Wilhelmina, my mother would've called you a caution."

Wilhelmina nodded. "Mine did."

Pastel grinned. "I intend to enjoy this evening."

"If you're hoping to land that Mr. Nordstrom, I think you got the right armor. Watch your virtue." She wrinkled her nose. "Don't suppose that matters much anymore."

"Yes, it does."

Wilhelmina pursed her lips. "I'll say this for ya. You fought for them kids. I was here to protect you, like Big Mike said I should. But you took on the job of taking care o'them." She jerked her head up and down. "I like that. Took guts. My mother would've liked you even if you do dress like a hussy."

"Uh . . . thank you." Grinning, Pastel snatched up the wrap that would cover her from head to foot. "We'll be late."

"Doesn't worry me."

"Don't wait up."

"I wouldn't. After Letterman, I'll be in bed."

Pastel was still laughing when she left the bedroom.

Anchor was waiting for her in the large sitting room downstairs. When he saw her, he rose from his chair and closed his eyes as though in pain. "I knew you'd wear it. I prayed you wouldn't."

Pastel chuckled. "Why?"

"You know why. You'll drive him crazy. And he'll glare at everyone."

"No, he won't."

"You knew what you were doing when you called and asked to wear it."

"Maybe."

"Don't let anything happen."

"Oh, I'll take care of the jewelry."

"That's not what I meant, and you know it." He shook his head. "You drove him nuts the first time he saw you in that."

Intrigued, Pastel let her purse drop to the couch. "Tell me."

"We haven't got time."

"Make it."

Anchor sighed. "He was in the sound booth.

You were under the lights. He went stiff as a board and didn't take his eyes from you. He canceled an important meeting with a high-profile client who always pays on time. You knocked him out."

"That's the idea."

Anchor winced. "Would you please marry the man and insure my job?"

"Will would never fire you."

"He might kill me when he sees you in that dress."

"Nonsense. We're going to a party." Laughing, she threw the coral wool wrapper lined in cream velvet over her dress. "See? I'm covered."

"I'm going to my execution," Anchor muttered, following her to the door.

"I'm just sorry Will got lassoed into having to take these new clients of yours to the Waldorf himself."

"Why they had to be escorted to this personally, I don't know. Will accommodated them, but they'd better not think they can jerk him around," Anchor told her as they left the house. "I don't like that kind of high-handedness. I think they're from one of those oil countries in the Middle East. Same kind of arrogance."

"Will can handle them."

"Yes . . . but it isn't like him to bend for something like this. Usually he sets down the schema, and they buy or don't."

"Maybe there was a reason they needed an escort."

"Maybe."

She inhaled the crisp night air. "Wonderful. Soon it'll be spring. My favorite time of the year."

The limousine provided by Will was comfortable and roomy.

Pastel felt very good about herself, about Will . . . about getting married as soon as possible. "If we're wed in Alaska, will you come, Anchor?"

"You couldn't keep me away. My mother's already up there."

Pastel laughed. "The Nordstroms are the greatest family for adopting other people's troubles."

Anchor nodded. "Thank goodness."

When they exited the limo, Anchor studied the driver.

"What's wrong?" Out of habit, Pastel scrutinized him too.

"I don't know. I generally know the drivers we use." He shrugged. "I guess I've gotten paranoid."

"I know the feeling."

"It looks beautiful," Pastel whispered as they stood at the entrance to the ballroom.

"It's a little cool. Maybe you should keep your wrap on, Pastel," Anchor said.

She turned to him, grinning. "Still worried about the boss."

"Damn straight. He'll have a coronary when he sees you."

The gloom in his voice had amusement bubbling out of her. "He won't blame you."

"No? Don't forget to block for me when he charges." Anchor jerked his head toward the room. "Speaking of himself."

Pastel didn't turn. Instead, she divested herself of the cloak and handed it to Anchor. Then she swung around to face Will.

He stopped dead in his tracks, his mouth falling open.

"Told ya," Anchor whispered.

"Don't worry," she muttered back.

"Pastel!"

He sounded unsure, miffed. She smiled. "Hi. Hope we're not late. Shall we join the others?"

"That dress."

"Great, isn't it. I told Anchor I was sure you wouldn't mind."

Will's gaze went past her to his assistant. "Is that right?"

"Yeah," Anchor said in a resigned tone.

"Don't blame him," Pastel said. "I insisted on wearing it."

"I don't blame Anchor. I know how persuasive you can be."

"Right." She beamed up at him.

"Why don't I feel more secure?" Anchor was talking to air as they moved away from him.

"You look beautiful," Will said through his teeth.

"Sounded like a condemnation to me, Nordstrom." She stopped, turning. "I love you, Will. Let's go in." She moved away.

Rooted to the ground, he looked after her.

Anchor came up to him. "Need something?"

"The strength to live with that woman."

Anchor smiled. "She is too beautiful . . . if that can be. She's just testing her powers on you. For some damn-fool reason, she didn't know she had any."

Will's smile twisted. "You read her right."

"She's a very good friend. I value her," Anchor said, his tone solemn. "Even though she drives me up a wall."

"Agreed."

"I think she's worth the anxiety."

"So do I." Will sighed. "Let's go. She has to have her little game with me."

"Yeah. I'd enjoy it more if I were sure you wouldn't tear the place apart. I wish your mother . . . or even my mother . . . were here."

Will glared at him. "I know how to behave."

Anchor looked after him as he stalked off. "Wish I believed that."

Pastel thought dinner was excellent. Braised snapper in endive was succulent, as were the side dishes, and the famous Caesar salad. The flambéed bananas in rum and liqueur were perfect.

"I enjoyed that," she said to Will, liking the idea of round tables rather than a head table with everyone facing it.

"Good."

When he smiled into her eyes, she all but slid off her chair to the floor.

The speeches took a while, but only one or two were boring.

When Will took the podium, Pastel could have burst with pride. He was a wonderful speaker, and people laughed and applauded, she louder than anyone.

When he returned to their table, she looked around at the people leaving their seats. "I think I'll chance the ladies' room before it gets too crowded."

Will made as if to go with her, and she put a hand on his arm. "You can't go to the ladies' room with me."

"I'll walk you over there. I like being with you."

They didn't make much headway across the room. Time after time they were stopped, and Will made introductions. They had almost reached the doors, when a man spoke at their backs.

"You must introduce me, Mr. Nordstrom."

They turned, and Pastel pulled back.

Will frowned at her. "What is it?"

"Nothing." Her smile was weak. "I'm sorry," she said to the dark-haired man. "I didn't catch your name."

"Said al Alar. I'm a businessman from Nahumi. We are to sign a contract with Nordstrom-Brockman on Monday. We hope to work with you and your models, Ms. Marx."

Pastel inclined her head, unable to speak. When had Will done this? Why hadn't he told her? Nahumi! Her skin crawled. Coincidence? Could be. She wasn't comfortable with that.

"I understand from what Mr. Nordstrom has told me, you have ties to my country."

"I did," Pastel said, the words barely pushing by her wooden lips. Who was he? Could this man know Ibn or his family? "If you gentlemen will excuse me, I'll find the rest room. No, please stay with Mr. al Alar. I'll be right back."

Not hearing what Will said to her, she turned and threaded her way out of the huge room as fast as she could. Once in the rest room, she stayed in the spacious outer area. White-faced, she stared at herself in the mirror. How long she stood there, she didn't know. When she noticed a woman eyeing her, she went into the other room and closed a cubicle door behind her. Using the facilities, she took deep breaths, getting herself in balance. Nahumi was not populated by villains. Many kind people lived there. She had to calm down.

When she exited the cubicle, the room had thinned of women. She washed her hands, then moved back to the outer room to freshen her makeup. Her hand shook so much, she could barely do it. When she was finally alone, she sighed with relief.

She heard the door behind her open and fumbled in her purse, not wanting to communicate by eye contact. She was on track. A few more minutes of solitude would help, though.

"You recognized me. I didn't think you would."

Pastel whirled around. "Mr. al Alar, this is for women only."

"Do not pretend, Miss Marx. Or should I say, 'Mrs.' Donnelly. It's over. The girls will go back to Nahumi with me."

Her worst nightmare enacted in a bathroom. The fates really had a macabre sense of humor.

"Who are you?"

He frowned. "I was wrong. I thought you saw the resemblance."

"You're not Ibn."

His frown deepened. "I am the fool's cousin."

"You can't stay in here. Someone will come."

"Don't be stupid." He jerked his head at the door. "My people are out there."

"Where is Pam?" The question was out before she could stop it.

He smiled, a frightening smile. "With her husband."

She couldn't speak; she could only stare at him.

"They're both dead," he continued. "Years ago. I suspected his wife knew where their daughters were, but Ibn wouldn't even let me talk to her. He had a change of heart too, decided he loved his girl children too much to barter them. He and his wife tried to leave Nahumi." Al Alar shrugged. "They never made it."

The anger and contempt in his voice tore at her. "You killed them."

He shrugged again. "We tried to honor our bond. The girls are what you Americans would call a bargaining chip. Once I found them again two years ago, I started renegotiating with the prince. The mineral rights he promised in exchange for Ibn's children would be very profitable for my family. Now we have come to terms. And I have come for the girls."

"You killed my friend!" Fury rocked her. "All those years, I didn't know. I tried to protect them . . . Pam . . . and Ibn and my girls." Pastel screamed, launching herself at him. "Bastard!" Surprise armed her. She kicked, driving her high-heeled shoe into his groin just as she'd been taught in a survival class she'd taken.

When al Alar grunted and doubled over, she smashed her fist into his nose.

His yell had the world erupting.

Will was there, lifting her away, hugging her for a moment, then handing her to Mike.

"Diplomatic immunity," al Alar gasped.

"Not from me," Will muttered.

The men were of equal girth. If Will was a little taller, al Alar was that much wider. Each was heavily muscled.

"Well matched," Anchor whispered.

Pastel rounded on him. "How can you say that. al Alar could hurt Will."

Anchor laughed. "No way."

Pastel paid no attention. Al Alar had just struck with his foot in the manner of eastern kick-boxing. It caught Will in the chest. She screamed and launched herself at the man.

Hard arms caught her around the waist.

She struggled. "Let me go. I have to help Will."

"He's doing fine. I'll get someone to take you out of here."

She wriggled around, glowering. "In your ear, Big Mike. I'm staying."

Several other men were crowded into the room, but Pastel barely noticed them. Her eyes were on Will and the man who struggled to kill him. An angry shout over by the door drew her attention, though, and she suddenly remembered something al Alar had said.

"There are others," she said to Mike.

"We've thought of that, Pastel." Mike patted her shoulder. "My people will've rounded them up."

"Do you ever use the police?" Worry made her query more acerbic than she wanted.

Mike smiled, sympathy in his eyes. "He'll be fine, you know. Will could wrestle a kodiak. Don't let the Brooks Brothers look fool you."

"I don't want him wrestling a kodiak," she muttered, her fingers threaded together.

The two men were lost in their own war. Nothing intruded on their concentration.

Will caught his opponent under the chin with a chop that would have dropped a horse. Al Alar staggered but didn't fall. Instead, he rushed Will.

Locked, stumbling, shoving for an opening, they swayed like two animals in a death struggle.

Pushed back, al Alar fumbled in his coat, bringing out a knife.

"No!" Pastel screamed.

It was a second of diversion. Enough. Will moved sideways, lifting his foot. He put everything he had behind the blow, catching al Alar in the jaw.

The crack had the assembled people grunting, in approval and not.

Al Alar dropped like a stone, facefirst on the carpet of the ladies' room.

"Our embassy will hear of this," a dark-visaged man held by one of Mike's people said.

Will swayed, blood oozing from his cut lip. "Sue me."

Pastel catapulted herself at him, flinging her arms around his waist. She turned on the speaker, furious, hungry for revenge. "Is that right? Well, our State Department is going to hear about the murder of the prime minister's son and his wife." She pointed a shaking finger at the unconscious al Alar. "He told me that he'd had them killed . . . my friend, Pam, and her husband." Biting back tears, she glared at al Alar's henchman.

"Your word against the people of my country," the man said.

"Not so." Anchor stepped forward, anger limning his features. "I remember you. You threatened my mother."

"Knock him down, or I will." Pastel tried to get to him.

Will held her. "He'll be taken care of." He stared at the man on the floor. "Every word he said was recorded on a little mike planted around my fiancée's neck."

Pastel touched the lavaliere at her throat.

Anchor waved a receiver at the man. "And I've got it all."

Al Alar's counterpart ground his teeth, attempting to lunge at Anchor. Strong hands manacled him.

Will looked at Mike. "You'll take care of this?" At the other's nod, he hugged Pastel. "Sorry, love, I'd better talk to some people before we go home."

"We're going to the hospital first," she announced. "Don't agrue."

"She's right," Anchor said. "Don't argue with her. She's mean."

Will laughed. Pastel made a face.

"I'll take care of the explanations, Will," Anchor said.

"Let's get out of here, lady love."

"I want you checked."

"Marry me, and you can check me every night."

They didn't leave right away. Policemen barred their way. Explanations had to be made, their IDs checked.

Once in the limo, Pastel was about to throw herself in his arms, but she caught herself. "You're hurt."

"Not that bad." Will hauled her close.

She was grinning when she happened to look at the huge driver who was watching them in the rearview mirror. "Will . . . ?"

"What?" He was busy nuzzling her neck, and trying not to wince when the contact stung his hurt mouth.

"The driver."

"Friend of mine—"

"From Alaska."

"Right." She was still laughing when he kissed her.

THIRTEEN

The wedding day had a beautiful May sheen. Alaska preened itself like a wondrous platter of jewels. Blue sky melded with the green glitter of earth, not quite sure if the hoarfrost should stay or go. A scudding cloud or two dashed past the sun to twist and turn in its azure path.

"Perfect day," Lars announced as he, Kort, Rafe, and Helborg followed Will into the church.

Will glared at them. "It should've been in March, in front of a JP."

They grinned.

"I've enjoyed this," Rafe whispered to his father-in-law. "Pays him back for all the times he made fun of me."

All but one of his in-laws, the bridegroom, chuckled.

———◈———————◈———

Pastel felt serene as she faced the aisle on Big Mike's arm. Althea and Yasmin beamed at her just before preceding her.

"A beautiful family," Mike whispered as the organ thundered out Mendelssohn and the assembled rose and turned. "And your girls love their new father."

"Yes," Pastel murmured, her eyes and mind on that man who waited for her at the altar. They moved forward in slow beat. She had time to nod to the smiling people. She glanced at Will. He was scowling. Swallowing a laugh, she inclined her head to Will's mother, and Aunt Adela in the front pew.

When she finally reached the altar, Will took her hand and looked into her eyes. "Pastel," he murmured.

"You're making an honest woman of me at last." She heard the chuckles behind her, the muffled amusement of his brothers, brother-in-law, and father.

Will shook his head, relaxing. "Let's do it, woman of mine."

The rest was a blur of music, vows, recessional, laughing congratulations.

The reception at the fire hall was fun.

"I love this," Pastel told Will as they whirled in

the lively folk dance that had called everyone onto the floor.

"You could get killed out here." Will glared at his sister Cassie, who whirled by with her husband, winking at him.

"I relish this, Will," Cassie called. "Revenge is sweet."

"What does she mean?" Pastel asked.

"I teased her and Rafe."

"Not anymore," Pastel said.

"We're leaving."

"In a bit."

Will looked around him, glancing at Yasmin and Althea, who were concentrating on learning the intricate steps. "Right. First I'll dance with my daughters."

Hours later they landed at a pristine lake tucked among hills and mountains in the Alaskan wilderness.

Pastel stepped out of the seaplane and gazed around her, astounded, enthralled. "It's wonderful. Where are we?"

"Theresa Lake. Not too many people know about it. It's not even on every map. My brothers and I came on it when we trekked this area as teenagers." Will smiled, touched and pleased at her wonder. "I like it."

"It's beyond imagining." She sighed when Will lifted her into his arms and stepped from the pontoon onto the treated wood dock. "Does it freeze over in the winter?" There was snow on the distant peaks.

"Most times it does. You can still see the ice on the west side." He tightened his hold, kissing her forehead.

She smiled up at him. "I'm glad you brought me here. It's perfect for us."

"I agree."

They entered the well-appointed log cabin, insulated in the Scandinavian fashion with wood walls and ceiling.

"Very cozy." Pastel felt a tremor go through him. She looked up at him. "Aren't you going to put me down?"

"Not ever."

His husky rejoinder melted her. "Will, I love you."

He let her slide down his body. "That keeps me going, wife."

She cupped his face with her hands. "Since our first meeting, it hasn't been easy. We've had more obstacles than a steeplechase. Not once have you faltered, stumbled, or retreated."

He grinned. "Not that you could see."

"Not once," she insisted. "You said the magic was in me." Her fingers caressed his face. "I think it's in you. And I want it for all time."

He leaned down, rubbing his lips over hers.

"We're married. We have a family. Nothing is better than this."

She cuddled close to him. "And we're alone."

"Shhh. Someone might hear you and drop in."

She chuckled, sliding her arms around his middle. "Not a chance."

He hugged her. "Maybe we could start work on an extension of our family." When she stiffened, he chucked her under the chin. "Just kidding."

"Too late."

He leaned back. "Meaning?"

"I'm expecting." When he staggered, she caught him around the waist. "Just barely. I really wasn't sure until today." The sheen of tears in his eyes made her teary. "It's wonderful, isn't it?"

"Wonderful." He kissed her hard and swung her up into his arms. "Just more of your magic, Pastel Nordstrom."

The spring sun crystallized the snow, and gold, diamonds, and emeralds cascaded over the fantasy Alaskan world. They embraced it all with their love.

THE EDITOR'S CORNER

Next month, LOVESWEPT is proud to present **CONQUERING HEROES,** six men who know what they want and won't stop until they get it. Just when summer is really heating up, our six wonderful romances sizzle with bold seduction and daring promises of passion. You'll meet the heroes of your wildest fantasies who will risk everything in pursuit of the women they desire, and like our heroines, you'll learn that surrender comes easily when love conquers all.

The ever-popular Leanne Banks gives us the story of another member of the Pendleton family in **PLAYING WITH DYNAMITE,** LOVESWEPT #696. Brick Pendleton is stunned when Lisa Ransom makes love to him like a wild woman, then sends him away! He cares for her as he never has another woman, but he just can't give her the promise that she insists is her dearest dream. Lisa tries to forget him, ignore him, but he's gotten under her skin, claiming her with every caress of his mouth and hands. The fierce demolition expert knows everything about tearing things down, but rebuilding Lisa's trust means fighting old demons—and confessing fear. **PLAYING WITH DYNAMITE** is another explosive winner from Leanne.

CAPTAIN'S ORDERS, LOVESWEPT #697, is the newest sizzling romance from Susan Connell, with a hero you'll be more than happy to obey. When marina captain Rick Parrish gets home from vacation, the last thing he expects to find is his favorite hang-out turned into a fancy restaurant by Bryn Madison. The willowy redhead redesigning her grandfather's bar infuriates him with her plan to sell the jukebox and get rid of the parrot, but she stirs long-forgotten needs and touches him in dark and lonely places. Fascinated by the arrogant and impossibly handsome man who fights to hide the passion inside him, Bryn aches to unleash it. This determined angel has the power to heal his sorrow and capture his soul, but Rick has to face his ghosts before he can make her his forever. This heart-stopping romance is what you've come to expect from Susan Connell.

It's another powerful story of triumph from Judy Gill in **LOVING VOICES**, LOVESWEPT #698. Ken Ransom considers his life over, cursing the accident that has taken his sight, but when a velvety angel voice on the telephone entices him to listen and talk, he feels like a man again—and aches to know the woman whose warmth has lit a fire in his soul. Ingrid Bjornson makes him laugh, and makes him long to stroke her until she moans with pleasure, but he needs to persuade her to meet him face-to-face. Ingrid fears revealing her own lonely secret to the man whose courage is greater than her own, but he dares her to be reckless, to let him court her, cherish her, and awaken her deepest yearnings. Ken can't believe he's found the woman destined to fill his heart just when he has nothing to offer her, but now they must confront the pain that has drawn them together. Judy Gill will have you laughing and crying with this terrific love story.

Linda Warren invites you to get **DOWN AND DIRTY**, LOVESWEPT #699. When Jack Gibraltar refuses to help archeology professor Catherine Moore find her missing aunt, he doesn't expect her to trespass on his turf, looking for information in the seedy Mexican bar! He admires her persistence, but she is going to ruin a perfectly good con if she keeps asking questions . . . not to mention drive him crazy wondering what she'll taste like when he kisses her. When they are forced to play lovers to elude their pursuers, they pretend it's only a game—until he claims her mouth with sweet, savage need. Now she has to show her sexy outlaw that loving him is the adventure she craves most. **DOWN AND DIRTY** is Linda Warren at her best.

Jan Hudson's conquering hero is **ONE TOUGH TEXAN**, LOVESWEPT #700. Need Chisholm doesn't think his day could possibly get worse, but when a nearly naked woman appears in the doorway of his Ace in the Hole saloon, he cheers right up! On a scale of one to ten, Kate Miller is a twenty, with hair the color of a dark palomino and eyes that hold secrets worth uncovering, but before he can court her, he has to keep her from running away! With his rakish eye patch and desperado mustache, Need looks tough, dangerous, and utterly masculine, but Kate has never met a man who makes her feel safer—or wilder. Unwilling to endanger the man she loves, yet desperate to stop hiding from her shadowy past, she must find a way to trust the hero who'll follow her anywhere. **ONE TOUGH TEXAN** is vintage Jan Hudson.

And last, but never least, is **A BABY FOR DAISY**, LOVESWEPT #701, from Fayrene Preston. When Daisy Huntington suggests they make a baby together, Ben McGuire gazes at her with enough intensity to strip the varnish from the nightclub bar! Regretting her impulsive words almost immediately, Daisy wonders if the man might just be worth the challenge. But when she finds an abandoned baby in her car minutes later, then quickly realizes that several dangerous men are searching for the child, Ben becomes her only hope for escape! Something in his cool gray eyes makes her trust him—and the electricity between them is too delicious to deny. He wants her from the moment he sees her, hungers to touch her everywhere, but he has to convince her that what they have will endure. Fayrene has done it again with a romance you'll never forget.

Happy reading,

With warmest wishes,

Nita Taublib

Nita Taublib

Associate Publisher

P.S. There are exciting things happening here at Loveswept! Stay tuned for our gorgeous new look starting with our August 1994 books—on sale in July. More details to come next month.

P.P.S. Don't miss the exciting women's novels from Bantam that are coming your way in July—**MISTRESS** is the newest hardcover from *New York Times* best-selling author Amanda Quick; **WILDEST DREAMS,** by best-selling author Rosanne Bittner, is the epic, romantic saga of a young beauty and a rugged ex-soldier with the courage to face hardship and deprivation for the sake of their dreams; **DANGEROUS TO LOVE,** by award-winning Elizabeth Thornton, is a spectacular historical romance brimming with passion, humor, and adventure; **AMAZON LILY,** by Theresa Weir, is the classic love story in the best-selling tradition of *Romancing the Stone* that sizzles with passionate romance and adventure as deadly as the uncharted heart of the Amazon. We'll be giving you a sneak peek at these terrific books in next month's LOVESWEPTs. And immediately following this page look for a preview of the exciting romances from Bantam that are *available now*!

Don't miss these extraordinary books by
your favorite Bantam authors

On sale in May:

DARK JOURNEY
by Sandra Canfield

SOMETHING BORROWED, SOMETHING BLUE
by Jillian Karr

THE MOON RIDER
by Virginia Lynn

"A master storyteller of stunning
intensity."
—*Romantic Times*

DARK JOURNEY
by Sandra Canfield

*From the day Anna Ramey moved to Cook's Bay, Maine,
with her dying husband—to the end of the summer when
she discovers the price of forbidden passion in another
man's arms, DARK JOURNEY is nothing less than
electrifying.* Affaire de Coeur *has already praised it as
"emotionally moving and thoroughly fascinating," and*
Rendezvous *calls it "A masterful work."*

Here is a look at this powerful novel . . .

"Jack and I haven't been lovers for years," Anna
said, unable to believe she was being so frank. She'd
never made this admission to anyone before. She
blamed the numbness, which in part was culpable,
but she also knew that the man sitting beside her
had a way of making her want to share her thoughts
and feelings.

Her statement in no way surprised Sloan. He'd
suspected Jack's impotence was the reason there
had been no houseful of children. He further suspected that the topic of discussion had something
to do with what was troubling Anna, but he let her
find her own way of telling him that.

"As time went on, I adjusted to that fact," Anna
said finally. She thought of her lonely bed and of

more lonely nights than she could count, and added, "One adjusts to what one has to."

Again Sloan said nothing, though he could painfully imagine the price she'd paid.

"I learned to live with celibacy," Anna said. "What I couldn't learn to live with was . . ."

Her voice faltered. The numbness that had claimed her partially receded, allowing a glimpse of her earlier anger to return.

Sloan saw the flash of anger. She was feeling, which was far healthier than not feeling, but again she was paying a dear price.

"What couldn't you live with, Anna?"

The query came so softly, so sweetly, that Anna had no choice but to respond. But, then, it would have taken little persuasion, for she wanted—no, needed!—to tell this man just how much she was hurting.

"All I wanted was an occasional touch, a hug, someone to hold my hand, some contact!" She had willed her voice to sound normal, but the anger had a will of its own. On some level she acknowledged that the anger felt good. "He won't touch me, and he won't let me touch him!"

Though a part of Sloan wanted to deck Jack Ramey for his insensitivity, another part of him understood. How could a man remember what it was like to make love to this woman, then touch her knowing that the touch must be limited because of his incapability?

"I reached for his hand, and he pulled it away." Anna's voice thickened. "Even when I begged him, he wouldn't let me touch him."

Sloan heard the hurt, the desolation of spirit, that lay behind her anger. No matter the circumstances, he couldn't imagine any man not responding to this woman's need. He couldn't imagine any man having the option. He himself had spent the better part of the morning trying to forget the gentle touch of her hand, and here she was pleading with her husband for what he—Sloan—would die to give her.

A part of Anna wanted to show Sloan the note crumpled in her pants pocket, but another part couldn't bring herself to do it. She couldn't believe that Jack was serious about wishing for death. He was depressed. Nothing more.

"What can I do to ease your pain?" Sloan asked, again so softly that his voice, like a log-fed fire, warmed Anna.

Take my hand. The words whispered in Anna's head, in her heart. They seemed as natural as the currents, the tides of the ocean, yet they shouldn't have.

Let me take your hand, Sloan thought, admitting that maybe his pain would be eased by that act. For pain was exactly what he felt at being near her and not being able to touch her. Dear God, when had touching her become so important? Ever since that morning's silken memories, came the reply.

What would he do if I took his hand?
What would she do if I took her hand?

The questions didn't wait for answers. As though each had no say in the matter, as though it had been ordained from the start, Sloan reached for Anna's hand even as she reached for his.

A hundred recognitions scrambled through two minds: warmth, Anna's softness, Sloan's strength, the smallness of Anna's hand, the largeness of Sloan's, the way Anna's fingers entwined with his as though clinging to him for dear life, the way Sloan's fingers tightened about hers as though he'd fight to the death to defend her.

What would it feel like to thread his fingers through her golden hair?

What would it feel like to palm his stubble-shaded cheek?

What would it feel like to trace the delicate curve of her neck?

What would it feel like to graze his lips with her fingertips?

Innocently, guiltily, Sloan's gaze met Anna's. They stared—at each other, at the truth boldly staring back at them.

With her wedding band glinting an ugly accusation, Anna slowly pulled her hand from Sloan's. She said nothing, though her fractured breath spoke volumes.

Sloan's breath was no steadier when he said, "I swear I never meant for this to happen."

Anna stood, Sloan stood, the world spun wildly. Anna took a step backward as though by doing so she could outdistance what she was feeling.

Sloan saw flight in her eyes. "Anna, wait. Let's talk."

But Anna didn't. She took another step, then another, and then, after one last look in Sloan's eyes, she turned and raced from the beach.

"Anna, please . . . Anna . . . *Ann-nna!*"

"Author Jillian Karr . . . explodes
onto the mainstream
fiction scene . . . Great reading."
—*Romantic Times*

SOMETHING BORROWED, SOMETHING BLUE
by
Jillian Karr

When the "Comtesse" Monique D'Arcy decides to
feature four special weddings on the pages of her
floundering *Perfect Bride* magazine, the brides find
themselves on a collision course of violent passions
and dangerous desires.

*The T.V. movie rights for this stunning novel have
already been optioned to CBS.*

The intercom buzzed, braying intrusively into
the early morning silence of the office.

Standing by the window, looking down at the sea
of umbrellas bobbing far below, Monique D'Arcy
took another sip of her coffee, ignoring the insistent
drone, her secretary's attempt to draw her into the
formal start of this workday. Not yet, Linda. The
Sinutab hasn't kicked in. What the hell could be so
important at seven-thirty in the morning?

She closed her eyes and pressed the coffee
mug into the hollow between her brows, letting
the warmth seep into her aching sinuses. The
intercom buzzed on, relentless, five staccato blasts

that reverberated through Monique's head like a jackhammer.

"Dammit."

She tossed the fat, just-published June issue of *Perfect Bride* and a stack of next month's galleys aside to unearth the intercom buried somewhere on her marble desk. She pressed the button resignedly. "You win, Linda. What's up?"

"Hurricane warning."

"*What?*" Monique spun back toward the window and scanned the dull pewter skyline marred with rain clouds. Manhattan was getting soaked in a May downpour and her window shimmered with delicate crystal droplets, but no wind buffeted the panes. "Linda, what are you talking . . ."

"Shanna Ives," Linda hissed. "She's on her way up. Thought you'd like to know."

Adrenaline pumped into her brain, surging past the sinus headache as Monique dove into her fight or flee mode. She started pacing, her Maud Frizon heels digging into the plush vanilla carpet. Shanna was the last person in the world she wanted to tangle with this morning. She was still trying to come to grips with the June issue, with all that had happened. As she set the mug down amid the organized clutter of her desk, she realized her hands were shaking. Get a grip. Don't let that bitch get the better of you. *Oh, God, this is the last thing I need today.*

Her glance fell on the radiant faces of the three brides smiling out at her from the open pages of the magazine, faces that had haunted her since she'd found the first copies of the June issue in a box beside her desk a scant half hour earlier.

Grief tore at her. Oh, God, only three of us. There were supposed to have been four. There *should* have been four. Her heart cried out for the one who was missing.

This had all been her idea. Four stunning brides, the weddings of the year, showcased in dazzling style. Save the magazine, save my ass, make Richard happy. All of us famed celebrities—except for one.

Teri. She smiled, thinking of the first time she'd met the pretty little manicurist who'd been so peculiarly reluctant at first to be thrust into the limelight. Most women dreamed of the Cinderella chance she'd been offered, yet Teri had recoiled from it. *But I made it impossible for her to refuse. I never guessed where it would lead, or what it would do to her life.*

And Ana, Hollywood's darling, with that riot of red curls framing a delicate face, exuding sexy abandon. Monique had found Ana perhaps the most vulnerable and private of them all. *Poor, beautiful Ana, with her sad, ugly secrets—I never dreamed anyone could have as much to hide as I do.*

And then there was Eve—lovely, tigerish Eve, Monique's closest friend in the world, the once-lanky, unsure teenage beauty she had discovered and catapulted to international supermodel fame. *All I asked was one little favor . . .*

And me, Monique reflected with a bittersweet smile, staring at her own glamorous image alongside the other two brides. Unconsciously, she twisted the two-and-a-half-carat diamond on her finger. Monique D'Arcy, the Comtesse de Chevalier. *If only they knew the truth.*

Shanna Ives would be bursting through her door any minute, breathing fire. But Monique couldn't stop thinking about the three women whose lives had become so bound up with her own during the past months. Teri, Ana, Eve—all on the brink of living happily ever after with the men they loved . . .

For one of them the dream had turned into a nightmare. *You never know what life will spring on you,* Monique thought, sinking into her chair as the rain pelted more fiercely against the window. *You just never know. Not one of us could have guessed what would happen.*

She hadn't, that long-ago dawn when she'd first conceived the plan for salvaging the magazine, her job, and her future with Richard. Her brilliant plan. She'd had no idea of what she was getting all of them into. . . .

THE MOON RIDER

by VIRGINIA LYNN

bestselling author of
IN A ROGUE'S ARMS

"Lynn's novels shine with lively adventures,
a special brand of humor
and sizzling romance."
—*Romantic Times*

*When a notorious highwayman accosted Rhianna and
her father on a lonely country road, the evening ended
in tragedy. Now, desperate for the funds to care for her
bedridden father, Rhianna has hit upon an ingenious
scheme: she too will take up a sword—and let the heart-
less highwayman take the blame for her robberies. But
in the blackness of the night the Moon Rider waits, and
soon this reckless beauty will find herself at his mercy,
in his arms, and in the thrall of his raging passion.*

"Stand and deliver," she heard the highwayman
say as the coach door was jerked open. Rhianna
gasped at the stark white apparition.

Keswick had not exaggerated. The highwayman
was swathed in white from head to foot, and she
thought at once of the childhood tales of ghosts
that had made her shiver with delicious dread.

There was nothing delicious about this apparition.

A silk mask of snow-white was over his face, dark eyes seeming to burn like banked fires beneath the material. Only his mouth was partially visible, and he was repeating the order to stand and deliver. He stepped closer to the coach, his voice rough and impatient.

Llewellyn leaned forward into the light, and the masked highwayman checked his forward movement.

"We have no valuables," her father said boldly. Lantern light glittered along the slender length of the cane sword he held in one hand. "I demand that you go your own way and leave us in peace."

"Don't be a fool," the Moon Rider said harshly. "Put away your weapon, sir."

"I have never yielded to a coward, and only cowards hide behind a mask, you bloody knave." He gave a thrust of his sword. There was a loud clang of metal and the whisk of steel on steel before Llewellyn's sword went flying through the air.

For a moment, Rhianna thought the highwayman intended to run her father through with his drawn sword. Then he lowered it slightly. She studied him, trying to fix his image in her mind so that she could describe him to the sheriff.

A pistol was tucked into the belt he wore around a long coat of white wool. The night wind tugged at a cape billowing behind him. Boots of white leather fit him to the knee, and his snug breeches were streaked with mud. He should have been a laughable figure, but he exuded such fierce menace that Rhianna could find no jest in what she'd earlier thought an amusing hoax.

"Give me one reason why I should not kill you on the spot," the Moon Rider said softly.

Rhianna shivered. "Please sir—" Her voice quivered and she paused to steady it. "Please—my father means no harm. Let us pass."

"One must pay the toll to pass this road tonight, my lovely lady." He stepped closer, and Rhianna was reminded of the restless prowl of a panther she'd once seen. "What have you to pay me?"

Despite her father's angry growl, Rhianna quickly unfastened her pearl necklace and held it out. "This. Take it and go. It's all of worth that I have, little though it is."

The Moon Rider laughed softly. "Ah, you underestimate yourself, my lady fair." He reached out and took the necklace from her gloved hand, then grasped her fingers. When her father moved suddenly, he was checked by the pistol cocked and aimed at him.

"Do not be hasty, my friend," the highwayman mocked. "A blast of ball and powder is much messier than the clean slice of a sword. Rest easy. I do not intend to debauch your daughter." He pulled her slightly closer. "Though she is a very tempting morsel, I must admit."

"You swine," Llewellyn choked out. Rhianna was alarmed at his high color. She tugged her hand free of the Moon Rider's grasp.

"You have what you wanted, now go and leave us in peace," she said firmly. For a moment, she thought he would grab her again, but he stepped back.

"My thanks for the necklace."

"Take it to hell with you," Llewellyn snarled. Rhianna put a restraining hand on his arm. The Moon Rider only laughed, however, and reached out for his horse.

Rhianna's eyes widened. She hadn't noticed the horse, but now she saw that it was a magnificent Arabian. Sleek and muscled, the pure white beast was as superb an animal as she'd ever seen and she couldn't help a soft exclamation of admiration.

"Oh! He's beautiful. . . ."

The Moon Rider swung into his saddle and glanced back at her. "I salute your perception, my fair lady."

Rhianna watched, her fear fading as the highwayman swung his horse around and pounded off into the shadows. He was a vivid contrast to the darker shapes of trees and bushes, easily seen until he crested the hill. Then, to her amazement, with the full moon silvering the ground and making it almost shimmer with light, he seemed to vanish. She blinked. It couldn't be. He was a man, not a ghost.

One of the footmen gave a whimper of pure fear. She ignored it as she stared at the crest of the hill, waiting for she didn't know what.

Then she saw him, a faint outline barely visible. He'd paused and was looking back at the coach. Several heartbeats thudded past, then he was gone again, and she couldn't recall later if he'd actually ridden away or somehow just faded into nothing.

And don't miss these fabulous romances from
Bantam Books, on sale in June:

MISTRESS
Available in hardcover
by *The New York Times* bestselling author
Amanda Quick
"Amanda Quick is one of the most versatile
and talented authors of the last decade."
—*Romantic Times*

WILDEST DREAMS
by the nationally bestselling author
Rosanne Bittner
"This author writes a great adventurous
love story that you'll put on
your 'keeper' shelf."
—*Heartland Critiques*

DANGEROUS TO LOVE
by the highly acclaimed
Elizabeth Thornton
"A major, major talent . . . a superstar."
—*Romantic Times*

AMAZON LILY
by the incomparable
Theresa Weir
"Theresa Weir's writing is poignant,
passionate and powerful."
—*New York Times*
bestselling author Jayne Ann Krentz

OFFICIAL RULES

To enter the sweepstakes below carefully follow all instructions found elsewhere in this offer.

The **Winners Classic** will award prizes with the following approximate maximum values: 1 Grand Prize: $26,500 (or $25,000 cash alternate); 1 First Prize: $3,000; 5 Second Prizes: $400 each; 35 Third Prizes: $100 each; 1,000 Fourth Prizes: $7.50 each. Total maximum retail value of Winners Classic Sweepstakes is $42,500. Some presentations of this sweepstakes may contain individual entry numbers corresponding to one or more of the aforementioned prize levels. To determine the Winners, individual entry numbers will first be compared with the winning numbers preselected by computer. For winning numbers not returned, prizes will be awarded in random drawings from among all eligible entries received. Prize choices may be offered at various levels. If a winner chooses an automobile prize, all license and registration fees, taxes, destination charges and, other expenses not offered herein are the responsibility of the winner. If a winner chooses a trip, travel must be complete within one year from the time the prize is awarded. Minors must be accompanied by an adult. Travel companion(s) must also sign release of liability. Trips are subject to space and departure availability. Certain black-out dates may apply.

The following applies to the sweepstakes named above:

No purchase necessary. You can also enter the sweepstakes by sending your name and address to: P.O. Box 508, Gibbstown, N.J. 08027. Mail each entry separately. Sweepstakes begins 6/1/93. Entries must be received by 12/30/94. Not responsible for lost, late, damaged, misdirected, illegible or postage due mail. Mechanically reproduced entries are not eligible. All entries become property of the sponsor and will not be returned.

Prize Selection/Validations: Selection of winners will be conducted no later than 5:00 PM on January 28, 1995, by an independent judging organization whose decisions are final. Random drawings will be held at 1211 Avenue of the Americas, New York, N.Y. 10036. Entrants need not be present to win. Odds of winning are determined by total number of entries received. Circulation of this sweepstakes is estimated not to exceed 200 million. All prizes are guaranteed to be awarded and delivered to winners. Winners will be notified by mail and may be required to complete an affidavit of eligibility and release of liability which must be returned within 14 days of date on notification or alternate winners will be selected in a random drawing. Any prize notification letter or any prize returned to a participating sponsor, Bantam Doubleday Dell Publishing Group, Inc., its participating divisions or subsidiaries, or the independent judging organization as undeliverable will be awarded to an alternate winner. Prizes are not transferable. No substitution for prizes except as offered or as may be necessary due to unavailability, in which case a prize of equal or greater value will be awarded. Prizes will be awarded approximately 90 days after the drawing. All taxes are the sole responsibility of the winners. Entry constitutes permission (except where prohibited by law) to use winners' names, hometowns, and likenesses for publicity purposes without further or other compensation. Prizes won by minors will be awarded in the name of parent or legal guardian.

Participation: Sweepstakes open to residents of the United States and Canada, except for the province of Quebec. Sweepstakes sponsored by Bantam Doubleday Dell Publishing Group, Inc., (BDD), 1540 Broadway, New York, NY 10036. Versions of this sweepstakes with different graphics and prize choices will be offered in conjunction with various solicitations or promotions by different subsidiaries and divisions of BDD. Where applicable, winners will have their choice of any prize offered at level won. Employees of BDD, its divisions, subsidiaries, advertising agencies, independent judging organization, and their immediate family members are not eligible.

Canadian residents, in order to win, must first correctly answer a time limited arithmetical skill testing question. Void in Puerto Rico, Quebec and wherever prohibited or restricted by law. Subject to all federal, state, local and provincial laws and regulations. For a list of major prize winners (available after 1/29/95): send a self-addressed, stamped envelope entirely separate from your entry to: Sweepstakes Winners, P.O. Box 517, Gibbstown, NJ 08027. Requests must be received by 12/30/94. DO NOT SEND ANY OTHER CORRESPONDENCE TO THIS P.O. BOX.